Why Am I Still Crying?

Shanta M. Collins

ENTEGRITY
CHOICE PUBLISHING

Why Am I Still Crying?
Copyright © 2016 Shanta M. Collins

Entegrity Choice Publishing
PO Box 453
Powder Springs, GA 30127
info@entegritypublishing.com

The views expressed in this work are solely those of the author and do not necessarily reflect the views of the publisher, and the publisher hereby disclaims any responsibility for them.

This is a work of fiction. All of the characters, names, incidents, organizations and dialogue in this novel are either products of the author's imagination or are used fictitiously.

Book Cover Designed by:
Kylie Dalton

ISBN: 978-0-9974859-0-5

Library of Congress Control Number: 2016954275

Printed in the United States of America

Dedication

This book is dedicated to those who have endured any form of abuse (physical, mental, emotional, or sexual) and to my beautiful daughters; Annequa Mitchell, Tamara Mitchell, Danielle Young and Lakendra Hale.

To those who believe their past abuse has canceled their future - your best is yet to come.

Do not take yesterday's mess into today's purpose and tomorrow's future.

Acknowledgments

Thank you, Lord, for sacrificing your son, Jesus Christ, for my sins and saving me. I am grateful that you kept me in spite of my sins.

Through life's turbulent journey, I felt your hand shielding me from my enemies who sought to do me harm. Thank you Lord for healing me physically, mentally, and spiritually and being with me at every turn in my life. When I rebelled, disobeyed, and forsook you, thank you for still loving me. Many times I wanted to give up and succumb to the pressures and temptations of suicide, but I felt you ministering to my spirit, causing me to fight on.

I am grateful for my mother Annette Mckinstry. We both have made mistakes, but I love her with all my heart.

A big thank you to my husband and my children for their patience and support. I could not have asked for a better family.

To the best mother and father-in-laws on this side of heaven, Leroy and Brenda Johnson; thank you for your love and support.

To B J, words cannot describe how much I appreciate your straight-forwardness, love, kindness, and support, when I wanted to quit. You are my teacher, friend, and a sister.

To my sister-in-Christ, Samantha Pegues, who is a prophetess, preacher, teacher, intercessor, and friend - bless you, Woman of God, for insisting that I take this four-year-old manuscript, tucked into my bookshelf inside a Kinko's bag, and get it published!

Contents

"Fear not; for thou shalt not be ashamed: neither be thou confounded; for thou shalt not be put to shame; for thou shalt forget the shame of thy youth, and shalt not remember the reproach of thy widowhood anymore. For thy Maker is thine husband; The Lord of hosts is his name; And thy Redeemer the Holy One of Israel; The God of the whole earth shall he be called. For the Lord hath called thee as a woman forsaken and grieved in spirit, and a wife of youth, when thou wast refused, saith thy God. For a small moment have I forsaken thee; but with great mercies will I gather thee. In a little wrath I hid my face from thee for a moment; but with everlasting kindness will I have mercy on thee, saith the Lord thy Redeemer." Isaiah 54:4-17

Introduction

I began writing this book in 2007. Since then, I have constantly had doubts about revealing such personal things about myself, even though I knew God was in it.

Instead of moving forward with publishing my book, I focused on other ventures, including returning to school to complete my RN degree (which I accomplished –thank you Lord). With that said, I truly hope and pray that my past chaos and mess blesses your soul; if you do not know Jesus Christ as your Lord and Savior, my hope is that my story brings you to know him. There is no other way to make it in this world we live in without Jesus Christ.

This book is about me and the countless episodes of abuse from the tender age of 4 years old until my young adult years. I was subjected to many of life's pains, rejections, and all types of abuse ranging from verbal, physical, and sexual in early childhood throughout my young adult years. I have lived a life of fear and low self-worth as a result of all the things I suffered.

I am going to take you on a journey through my life past and present. I sincerely hope and pray that you will be able to learn from my mistakes.

Someone once told me, "Shanta, you will not live long enough to make every mistake in life, so you have to learn from others' mistakes as well." I have taken this with me and applied it to my life; and, yes, I have still made some mistakes but not as many as I would have without trying to learn from others. I don't want you to think that you will not make any mistakes, but I hope you will not make the same ones I made.

I have to give thanks to Jesus Christ for loving me when no one else did and seeing me through his eyes and not the eyes of man. I did not get to where I am today alone; God carried me all the way. This book is divinely inspired. It was so difficult recalling past pains and mistakes, but I made it through. I can truly say that when I look back over my life and see all that God has done for me, my soul cries, "Hallelujah! I thank God for saving me." God gave me this book at a time when I thought that my life was just right.

But, I continued to have moments and times of depression. Often, I prayed and asked the Lord, "Why am I still crying, if I have been delivered?"

Many times I became depressed and withdrawn, and eventually it affected my marriage. I was like a schizophrenic person, happy at times and sad the next, for no apparent reason. During my bouts of depression, the enemy (satan), would rehearse my past in my head and tell me that I could not be who God said I was. The constant attacks drained me spiritually and made me ineffective to those around me. I was trying to live my life according to God's will. I prayed constantly three to four times a day. When everyone in the house was in the bed sleeping, I was up praying.

I constantly read and studied my Bible; nevertheless, I could not figure out what was the problem. After crying and feeling down for months, I heard the Lord speak to me early one morning, he told me to let go of my past. You see, I had never really let go of my past; I had only suppressed it, so it would come back whenever a problem arose in my life. In fact, I had not been truly delivered; residue of my past lingered. Do you see any residue of your past?

The Lord instructed me to write this book and confirmed that he would indeed heal me from my past. God reminded me that the things I went through in life were never just about me but for the sole purpose of him getting the Glory from my life and to lift up someone else.

The purpose of this book is to encourage anyone who is struggling to overcome the present or past pains and memories of abuse (sexual, verbal, and physical), teen pregnancy, promiscuity, high school dropout, continual rejection, and failed marriages. This book may not appeal to you if you have not endured these situations, but you may know someone who has.

This is my story, but I hope it serves as a guide and support to those who need it and want to be completely delivered from the depressing feelings associated with their experiences.

My prayer is that this book blesses many, but I will be just as happy if it blesses and restores one soul. This is not intended to be another self-help book, but a Christ-help book! We cannot help ourselves without first submitting to God and accepting Jesus Christ into our life; He is our help. This book is God's ministry.

You are not victims but victorious in all that you do. By the end of this book, I pray that you are able to forgive what others have done to you (Ephesians 4:32), forgive yourself for your mistakes (Philippians 3:13), believe that God has truly forgiven you, and act on it (Isaiah 43:25)!

"Get wisdom, get understanding: forget it not; neither decline from the words of my mouth. Forsake her not, and she shall preserve thee: love her, and she shall keep thee." Proverbs 4:5-6

1
Rewind To The Beginning

Allow me to tell you a little about myself. I am the mother of nine and the eldest of four siblings. I have been a Licensed Practical Nurse for ten years. My hobbies include reading, talking, and singing. I enjoy comedy because I like laughter. My greatest joy is serving others; if I am not helping someone else I feel as if I am not fulfilling my purpose in life. I have been shy since childhood. I am talkative, depending upon whom I am talking to; I have trust issues so I don't talk much unless I know you. I like to joke and laugh a lot; my daughters tell me, I laugh too much.

On a more serious note, I am an honest and up-front person, but I have found that everyone who asks for honesty does not truly want you to be honest. Your honesty can reveal your enemies real fast. I have tried to sugar coat things, but that does not work for me. I am very often misunderstood. I am loving, kind, generous, too generous, according to my husband. I am that person whom everyone calls when there is a problem or they need advice. I used to wonder why people chose to ask me for advice when I had just as many problems as they but I stopped wondering and started thanking God for giving me the wisdom to help. I just look and smile when my elders (and by elders I mean those that are older than me) tell me how much wisdom and knowledge I have.

From the beginning…Shortly after my birth, my mother moved to Montgomery, Alabama, where she had met my father. My father was not around for long; he told me he left when I was about a year old. I do not have any memories of him, for the longest time I did not know how he looked until now, at the age of 34, I received a picture from him by email.

My childhood was anything but perfect, but I have some fun memories of playing with my cousins and doing some of the craziest things. I remember the time my mom was washing clothes at the laundry house and for some strange reason I decided to drink some bleach. I got sick, but I can't recall what happened after that. I can also recall the time my cousins and I were jumping off the tables at the laundry house. I wanted to see who could jump the farthest so I put a wagon in front of the table (the little red wagons we had back then). It was my last jump. I was taken to the hospital for sutures because I landed on my chin; I still have that scar.

The part of my childhood I have tried so hard to suppress (but it continues to come back whenever I enter into my depressed mode) involves the acts of sexual abuse I endured. I was about four years old at the time. A male friend of my mother would babysit when she went out on the weekends. These memories are very clear; I remember being awakened out of my sleep, and he would make me perform sexual acts and touch him on his private parts.

At that age I had no idea what I was doing, but I knew that I did not like it. I would cry the entire time. I can still recall the smell of his clothes; it made me sick and, strangely enough, I can even close my eyes now and smell the scent.

One day my mother asked me if he was doing anything to me. Honestly, because I was so young at the time, I don't remember my response, but I always felt as though she knew. Why else would she have asked? Well, the day she asked me that question, I thought I would never see him again, but I did later when I was eight years old.

When I was about eight years old, we moved into a new apartment complex. My brother was four. I had the worst case of sibling jealousy; I remember having some hateful feelings toward my brother. The only friends we had were my mother's co-workers children. My mom continued to party but she started going to church occasionally with her friends, whom I came to call my aunts. They were the only family I knew because my mother's family lived in Mobile, AL. My mother provided us with everything we needed from a material standpoint. She made sure we did not lack in that area.

I know now that being a single parent isn't easy. We had all the material things we needed, but I was lacking emotional care and support. Well, my mother continued to go to the club but not as often. The day when I met my past again was when my mom and aunts went out together for the evening, and again my mother's friend volunteered to babysit. He would hug me and treat me like I was his favorite child in front of her, but, like before, when everyone went to sleep he would awaken me and repeat the same acts of sexual abuse. (Yes, I intentionally left out the details; I have no desire to feed anyone's flesh.) My reaction was the same as before, I just cried myself to sleep. I never said anything. Why? FEAR!

Over time my mom met the man who became my first step-father. He was good to us and gave me and my brother anything we wanted. The wedding was beautiful, and my mom was happy. As time went by however, things changed; the fighting began. He would beat my mom often. One night my brother and I were in our room asleep, and in the middle of the night we were awakened to hear my mother crying and a lot of yelling; he was beating her.

I thought that he was going to push her down the stairs that night. We ran out of the room and my brother hit my stepdad in the back, yelling at him to stop hitting my mom. I just stood back, crying. What we did not know at the time was that my stepfather had started doing drugs and drinking. One night the police kicked the door of our apartment in. My stepfather apparently had been selling drugs, and he and some other guys had burglarized an elderly couple and killed them. My mom was accused as well because they found drugs in the apartment.

My mom's life was saved by the grace of God. The church where we had been visiting spoke on behalf of my mother, and the state decided not to press any charges. Shortly afterwards, we joined the church and accepted Christ. I can remember that day clearly. It was a small Holiness church; they would sit the folding chairs at the front of the altar for anyone who desired to join and for salvation. I was eight years old then. My stepdad, of course, was incarcerated, and my mom got a divorce. Although he was an abusive man, he was all the father figure that I had at that time. In my eyes when he came into the picture the sexual abuse ended, so I missed him. Oddly enough, he was my security blanket.

2

Sexual Abuse

The National Center on Child Abuse and Neglect defines child sexual assault as: "Contacts or interactions between a child and an adult when the child is being used for sexual stimulation of the perpetrator or another person when the perpetrator or another person is in a position of power or control over the victim."

Sexual abuse is any time that a child is engaged in a sexual situation with an older person. It can include actual physical contact, such as fondling or rape, but it also includes making a child watch sexual acts or pornography, using a child in any aspect of the production of pornography, or making a child look at an adult's genitals.

Examples of child sexual abuse: Digital (finger) penetration; Exhibitionism; Fondling a child's genitals; Having intercourse with a child; Having oral sex with a child; Having sex in front of a child; Having a child touch an older person's genitals; Incest; Masturbation; Oral-genital contact; Prostitution; Rape; Showing an adult's genitalia to a child; Showing X-rated books or movies to a child; Sodomy; Using a child in pornographic production of any kind.

Many experts believe that sexual abuse is the most under-reported form of child maltreatment because of the secrecy or "conspiracy of silence" that so often characterizes these cases.

The Progression of the Act: *Excerpted from Delaplane, D. and A. Delaplane. Victims of Child Abuse, Domestic Violence, Elder Abuse, Rape, Robbery, Assault, and Violent Death: A Manual for Clergy and Congregations. Special Edition for Military Chaplains.*

There are usually several stages in the process of sexual victimization of children.

1.   The Approach

Child sexual abuse (molestation) is an intentional activity. The first requirement (with rare exceptions) is that the offender be alone with the child.

The child is often induced into being alone with the perpetrator by his suggestion of some activity like playing a game. It should be kept in mind that the greatest number of child molestations are by someone known to the child. Even in cases of "strangers" (those outside the family context) the offender, after becoming acquainted with the mother or caretaker, may offer to spend some time with the child in sports, a trip to the zoo, or museum.

The initial approach (coming from an adult who may be the father, step-father, or another known person who says it is okay), usually results in a favorable response. This is because children tend to accept adult authority, particularly from adults closest to them. In such cases, the warnings about not talking with strangers do not seem relevant.

One exception to this trust factor on the part of the child is when the child has been molested, and this is a repeat request. In this event, the child may back off, but by then the "secret," with accompanying warnings, has already been established. The game itself turns out to be "our little secret." It is presented as a very special game. It may take the form of, "Look at my penis. Do you want to touch it? Its fun, isn't it? When we are finished, we'll go out and have ice cream."

There is, unfortunately, another method which does not involve this kind of fun and gentleness. Force, intimidation, threats, and duress are used by some less skilled or deviant perpetrators. In these cases, the threat may be taken very seriously by the child because of her/his having seen force used on the mother or another in the family. Although sexual molestation, regardless of the method of approach, is very confusing and traumatic to the child, the forced molestation results in extreme trauma because of the additional intense fear factor.

2.   Sexual Interaction

Child molestation, like other addictive behaviors, is progressive. It may start with touching or fondling but can progress to some form of penetration --vaginal, oral, anal, or all three.

3. Secrecy

Keeping the secret is absolutely necessary in order to avoid consequences and to allow continued availability to the victim. The longer the secret is held, the longer the behavior is able to continue. The offender usually knows that this conduct is against the law and is, therefore, not averse to telling the child that bad things will happen if the secret gets out. Violent offenders may be more specific, telling the child that bad things will happen to her/him if the secret is told. Many wonder why children do not tell. This threat aspect is the reason.

Children will usually keep the secret unless the confusion and pain is too great, or unless it is accidentally revealed. Many never tell or do not disclose the secret until years later. To some, the experience is so shameful and traumatic that they actually forget (or block) the experiences. When other problems arise in adulthood, therapists often find, to the surprise of the victim, that childhood molestation which was blocked is at the root of the present problems.

4. Disclosure

Often disclosure is not voluntary. It may come through a slip of the child. She/he may unintentionally tell a playmate, a day care provider, a Sunday or Sabbath school teacher, or other teacher or caretaker. Or disclosure may come by observation. There are many indicators of possible sexual assault; the presence of a number of these could cause suspicion. There are also cases where the disclosure is voluntary. The small child may be so traumatized or in such confusion that she/he must get it out. The child may do this indirectly by making it sound like the molestation is happening to someone else. Or she/he may just drop a word or two about it in the middle of a completely unrelated conversation. It is very important for adults close to the child to hear these words and, without any emotional reaction (a very difficult assignment), to draw the child out further. If there is a strong reaction on the part of the adult listener, the child's fear may cause her/him to close down.

When a child molestation victim reaches adolescence, she/he may be so distraught by the ongoing molestation that she/he will voluntarily disclose it. Disclosure will often be to the non-offending parent, to a trusted member of the family, or, in some cases, it may even be to the authorities.

Whether the disclosure is voluntary or involuntary, there will be immediate reactions by the offender ranging from denial and hostility to a desire to obtain help. The first line of defense for the offender is, of course, denial. This can be very strong and convincing. There is a lot at stake. There are severe consequences to admission but even more severe ones if not admitted and later found to be true by the courts. Publicity, loss of reputation, criminal charges, financial difficulties, and marital and family breakdown are all possible outcomes which give strong motivation for the offender to lie.

Thus, the offender may, in his position as an adult authority, attempt to undermine the victim's account. In a debate between an articulate adult and a child, the child, unless believed, can often come out the loser... in more ways than one.

Non-offending spouses, on the other hand, must also deal with important issues. The first is whether to believe the alleged offender. If the allegations are accepted as true, in addition to the above listed consequences, she must deal with the possible loss of financial security, the possibility of having to testify against her husband or partner, or perhaps even being victimized herself by physical or other forms of retaliation.

Also, the non-offending spouse may feel guilt for not protecting the child. In the process of looking the other way for fear it might be true, she may have known and yet not known. Always the question in the minds of everyone involved in the disclosure phase is, "How will I be affected by this?"

This leads to, perhaps, the most important question of all -- to report or not report. In the case of involuntary disclosure, the suspicion of child molestation may come from someone who is mandated by law to report. In this case, the decision is taken out of the hands of the family members.

Although it is very difficult to see the law, social services, or the courts involved, reporting can be a very positive step toward resolution of the problem. First and foremost, it will alert those who can protect the victim. In addition, it may bring about accountability and the possibility of treatment for the victim and often for the offender, particularly if admission and cooperation are forthcoming.

Clergy can play a very important part by reporting if they suspect child abuse, by encouraging the offender to overcome denial and seek treatment, and by assisting all parties involved through the system, keeping the welfare of the victim as a paramount concern.

5. Suppression

It is very common, in view of all of the problems surrounding disclosure, for all parties involved to attempt, or at least consider, suppression. Even in the less likely event of the offender being an outsider, there is the strong temptation to try to avoid publicity and intervention. This is often done by minimization -- the attitude that, "It's not as big a deal as all that. She'll soon get over it." But she won't.

As the victim, the offender, and the non-offending parent or family member become involved in the investigation and the court process, the offender may very well seek to discredit the child by pointing out both factual and fictitious faults of the victim. These may be such things as the victim's difficulty in school (which is not unusual for a victim of molestation) or her/his tendency to lie. This can cause a child, who may already be having problems with guilt, to feel isolated. She/he may simply stop cooperating with the investigation. The child might even change her story to get back into good graces.

6.   Repression or Recovery

This is the choice. If the child sexual assault is suppressed, some surface adjustments may be made and life will go on as before. In most cases, "as before" will involve all that went on before, including the continued molestation. Having gotten away with it, the offender may begin to molest another child as well. The dysfunction is perpetuated.

Moving toward recovery, perhaps initially the more difficult alternative is by all standards the preferred choice. Treatment of both the child victim, who has been severely damaged, and of the offender, who struggles with deep-seated psychological difficulties, is long and difficult. More often than not, treatment will last up to two years and possibly more. Often the specter of being required to return to court if treatment is not maintained is the only incentive that will keep the offender in treatment.

If those involved will not give up when things "die down" or appear "normal" again, the reward of a young person's not having to live with this darkness and of the offender's finally acknowledging and dealing with his problem, is worth it all.

Child's Appearance:

Has torn, stained, or bloody underclothing; Experiences pain or itching in the genital area; Has bruises or bleeding in external genitalia, vagina, or anal regions; Has a sexually transmitted disease; Has swollen or red cervix,

23

vulva, or perineum; Has semen around mouth or genitalia or on clothing; Is pregnant.

Child's Behavior:
Appears withdrawn or engaged in fantasy or infantile behavior; Begins wetting or soiling the bed; Has poor peer relationships; Is unwilling to participate in physical activities; Is engaging in delinquent acts; Reports sexual abuse; Engages in inappropriate sexualized behavior; Devalues sexual acts and acts sexually permissive; Fears a certain person or certain places; Gives an unusual or unexpected response when asked if he or she was touched by someone; Has an unreasonable fear of a physical exam; Creates drawings that show sexual acts or that seem overly focused on sexual body parts; More knowledge about sex than is normal for the child's age; Pain, bruising, or bleeding in the genitals; Seems preoccupied with or overly concerned about sexual acts and words; Runs away.

Caretaker's Behavior:
Extremely protective or jealous of child; Encourages child to engage in prostitution or sexual acts; Has been sexually abused as a child; Is experiencing marital difficulties; Misuses alcohol or other drugs; Is frequently absent from home; Has difficulty in interacting emotionally with adults.

Effects of Child Abuse on Children: Sexual Abuse

The strongest indicators that a child has been sexually abused are inappropriate knowledge about sex, inappropriate sexual interest, and sexual acting out. The effects of abuse result from the abuse itself, from the family's response to the situation, and from the stigmatization that accompanies abuse. The symptoms can include post-traumatic symptoms, precocious sexualization, depression, anxiety, guilt, fear, sexual dysfunction, dissociative symptoms, eating disorders, substance abuse, prostitution, regressive behaviors such as a return to thumb-sucking or bed-wetting, runaway behavior, and academic and behavior problems.

Factors that influence the outcomes in cases of childhood sexual abuse include the age of the victim, the frequency and extent of the abuse, the relationship of the victim to the abuser (incest has the worst outcomes), the use of force, the presence of severe injury, and the number of different perpetrators. The response of the victim's family has a tremendous effect on the outcome. Supportive responses from the victim's family and friends can go far to lessen the impact of the abuse while negative responses (seen commonly in cases of incest where one parent tries to protect the other parent) will compound the damage done.

Effects of Child Abuse on Adults: Childhood Sexual Abuse

A history of childhood sexual abuse leads to a lower health-related quality of life and a greater number of health problems, psychiatric symptoms, and diagnoses. Research shows that survivors of childhood sexual abuse have "more medical problems, higher medical use, more physical symptoms, lower health status, and more medical procedures". High levels of anxiety and depression in survivors of childhood sexual abuse can lead to self-destructive behaviors, such as alcohol and drug abuse. Because of the association between sexual behavior and pain and violation, survivors of childhood sexual abuse often develop problems with intimate relationships in general, including difficulties during sexual contact and dysfunctions of desire and arousal.

In general, childhood sexual abuse is associated with a greater risk of: Disturbances in sexual interest; Difficulties during sexual contact; Dysfunctions of desire, arousal or orgasm; Seductive behaviors, compulsive activity and prostitution; Precocious sexual behavior; Confusion of sexuality and nurturing behavior; Sexually transmitted diseases; Unintended pregnancy; Eating disorders; Excessive weight gain; Depression; Anxiety; Self-destructive behavior; Alcoholism; Drug abuse; Panic attacks; Insomnia and sleep problems; Relationship problems; Revictimization; Suicide; Self-mutilation; Increased risk for sexually transmitted disease; Identity disturbances; and Involvement in physically abusive relationships as adults.

Sexual Abuse Injuries

There are no medical signs in the vast majority of sexual abuse cases. Several physical injuries are strong signs of sexual abuse. The oral cavity is a frequent site of sexual abuse in children. The presence of oral and perioral gonorrhea or syphilis in prepubescent children is a strong sign of sexual abuse. When gonorrhea or syphilis is diagnosed in a child, the case must be reported to public health authorities for investigation of the source and other contacts. Bite marks are lesions that may indicate sexual abuse. Gags applied to the mouth may leave bruises, scratching, or scarring at the corners of the mouth.

Many abuse survivors are highly competent in their professional and personal lives, compensating for the adverse effects of an abusive childhood until some added stress is introduced, perhaps a physical illness, birth of a child, or the death of a family member.

Beyond the obvious effects of child abuse (physical injury and stress-related physical ailments), victims of emotional, physical, sexual, and verbal abuse experience psychological damage that can last a lifetime. The results of abuse may include chronic depression, anxiety, behavior problems, problems in school - the list goes on and on.

> *"But Jesus said, suffer little children, and forbid them not, to come*
> *Unto me: for of such is the kingdom of heaven." Matthew 19:14*

By the time I was ten years old, we had moved into our first home; we were so excited! Finally, my brother and I no longer had to share rooms. We started a new school, which was intimidating for me. I was so timid it was difficult to make friends, and when you are timid, you tend to get bullied around. I stayed to myself; if you did not talk to me, then I did not talk to you.

As for my past abuse, I suppressed it as though it never happened. We were going to church every Sunday morning and evening, Wednesday, and Thursday nights. I was in the choir and my brother played the drums. The church became our family, and being so involved in church helped to further bury my past. My mom became close friends with our pastor's daughter. You would not think that anything was wrong with that, but it became a problem.

Eventually "cliques" formed in the church among the women, and it was always a tug of war concerning who was closer to whom and who dressed better than who. In the midst of this confusion, the people in the church began to talk and accuse the pastor of favoritism. An issue arose with me singing in the choir and wearing pants. Because it was a holiness church, we were supposed to wear dresses or skirts only. I was given the option to leave the choir or stop wearing pants. Being a young child, I should not have had to make such a choice, but I did. My mom let me decide, so I stepped down from the choir. It was too cold in the winter to wear skirts and dresses all the time. After that incident, I looked everywhere in the Bible to find where it said that I could not wear pants, but I never found that scripture. But what it did say was that women should not wear anything that pertains to men and vice versa. Over time I was given the okay to return to the choir but after some time, I was again asked to step down.

Things in church turned ugly when my mom became pregnant. She was not married, and the father was married. She was talked about and preached about. I had to stop talking to my friends in church because their parents were mad at my mom. I did not know how my mom's actions made others resent me. Church was the only stability I had at that time in my life. My mom left our church whenever she got mad.

Due to the conflict at my home church, we began attending a different church. The pastor at our new church was a prophet, or so he said. It was at this church that I encountered my next abuser, the pastor's son. I'm not sure if there is anything more traumatizing than being abused sexually at the hands of the son of a pastor. I was very uncomfortable going to church and telling my mom about the abuse was not an option.

Every decision my mother made affected me and my brother. When she was mad at the people at church or at work, she brought it home and we felt her wrath. The verbal and emotional abuse came directly from my mother.

I believed that church was my safe haven, but after being put out of the choir, mom's constant church hopping, and suffering abuse from the pastor's son, church was not safe anymore.

I endured my last act of sexual abuse when my mother left me and my brother with her co-worker's son who took advantage of me as well. All this abuse just became normal to me. Apparently I asked for it or so I thought. I implore parents to watch your children and know beyond any doubt that you are leaving the care of your child with a safe person.

3
My Preteen Years

Over time my mom ran into some financial problems. Our home was foreclosed, and our things were put out on the street. We had to move in with a friend, and after that we moved to boarding homes that housed college students. Life was hard. My mother was always unhappy. I remember the day we lost our home, and my mom said that she would never be happy again; well, she has not been. Be careful what you speak out of your mouth and into your life. She never had anything good to say to me, and I would get beatings for no reason just because she was hurt. My life consisted of babysitting my younger brother and going to school.

Occasionally I would have to stay home from school to babysit. I maintained good grades in school by the grace of God. I was in and out of trouble in school and was suspended a couple of times for fighting. I recall starting at least one of those fights. When I made it to junior high/middle school, I focused on school, and my good times were at school. School became my escape from the world at home. Moving from place to place and going from church to church, church was no longer a reliable source of protection for me.

Mom continued to take care of us the best she could, but emotionally I was damaged goods. I became interested in boys by the time I was twelve. My interest in boys is where I got attention.

Because of the degrading things my mom would say to me, I felt unloved and unwanted. I tried to tell my mother what I was feeling, so I decided to write her a letter since I could not talk to her without getting yelled at. Well, that did not help; she just yelled and cursed me. So I gave up talking to her. I would talk to other adults if I had a problem or questions about life; otherwise, I just held everything inside. My godmother was my closest friend.

At school I would lie about where we lived because I was embarrassed to tell anyone. When I got involved with sports in school, it was a hassle for my mother, so I would have to quit or find my own way home from school. I spent most of my time taking care of my siblings. I remember listening to my godmother and her sisters talking about how much time I spent babysitting. I heard one of them say, "I bet she will be pregnant by next year." I was eaves dropping and certainly did not understand how babysitting would lead to me getting pregnant. Later I realized that it was not babysitting but the fact that I was growing up alone without any true guidance at home that could lead to pregnancy.

My New Stepfather

My mom began to do prison ministry with some friends that she had met at another church. She got involved in a relationship with a prisoner that was opposed by almost everyone. My pastor disapproved, and so did my grandmother (my mom's mother). But she was in love and wanted to marry this man. My pastor refused to perform the ceremony initially, but eventually he did. My pastor had married so many people who ended in divorce that he no longer wanted to marry anyone who was not saved; he wanted the couples to be "equally yoked." Well, the day came and they were married. He was released from prison shortly afterwards, some say with the help of my mother and pastor.

We moved into a house after that. This house was located behind the projects where my father's family lived. I did not know many people there but I made friends soon. My mother was happy, I guess, but she was still upset because of the talk about her marrying a man out of prison. My grandmother never came to the wedding, and she stopped speaking to my mom. I was the one that had to deal with my mother's attitude and verbal abuse.

Sometimes people lash out at the person closest to them because they do not have the courage to stand up to whomever they are upset with or they do not know how to communicate effectively. My mom had both of these problems. Since no one cared for my new stepfather, she felt as if I did not either. But little did she know it did not make a difference to me either way. I remember the time he gave me $20 as allowance. My mother had never given me allowance before so I was excited. Well, I lost the money and my mom became irate and beat me, claiming that I lost the money intentionally because I did not like him. Even if I did not like him, I would not throw away money.

Things were fine for a while until the fighting began. I would listen to them fight about my mom not spending enough time with him, among other things. She had to work all the time since he was not working. What did he expect? One day while they were arguing he threatened to hit her; I overheard and went to her defense. He got up and left the house for a while. Well, the next day things were as if nothing happened. Some weeks following that, he checked me out of school because we had been having some plumbing problems and he said he needed me to wait for the plumber. Well, when we arrived home, I waited in my room for the plumber; he was in their room.

He called me into their room and asked me to sit next to him. I did and he started telling me how my mother did not spend enough time with him; he placed his hands on my legs and said, "I know you need attention just like I do." I jumped up off the bed and grabbed the fingernail file that was on the dresser and threatened to kill him if he ever touched me again. I called my godmother, and she called my mother. My mom and my pastor's wife picked me up from the house. They asked me what happened and I told them. Well, my mother's comment to my pastor's wife was that she could not believe me because I had been getting into trouble in school. I sat there and cried. She didn't even believe me. After that it was just swept under the rug, like everything else. After nights of arguing and fighting, he finally left my mom alone and pregnant.

Headed Down the Wrong Road

Times became even more difficult. The marriage everyone opposed and warned Mom about did not last. My mom said that it was my fault that he left. I began acting out after he left. I began to hang with the wrong crowd of people, mostly people that were older than me. I lost my virginity at the age of twelve. The experience was not pleasurable, but I liked the attention I received from him. For the sake of protecting this person's identity, I will call him Bill.

Bill showed care and concern almost like a father figure; he was four years older than me. My mom had a talk with me when I got my first period and explained to me that I could get pregnant, so I was not to have sex. She forgot to tell me not to fall for the lies that the boys tell to get what they want. I cannot blame losing my virginity on my mom because she said no sex, but I disobeyed. The relationship did not last long at all. Soon he acted as if he did not even know me.

My godmother heard that I was having sex; she called and asked me if I wanted to get on birth-control. I denied it to the end. She never told my mother, but she continued to try to get me to take the pills, but I could not tell her that I was having sex.

Soon afterwards, I began to stay out all night. I heard the rumors about me in the neighborhood, but I did not care. I was just trying to fit in with everyone else. And all the other girls were doing it before me. Starting at twelve, I had become promiscuous and carrying myself like an adult, but mentally I was far from being an adult. My godmother cut ties with me because she said I was too fast. But the problem wasn't that I was fast but that I was looking for affection in the wrong places. No one knew how hard it was living with a mother that did not care about you or even showed any love. You see, I had mistaken sex for love and intimacy. There was no one around to teach me differently. I did not have church as my mother had left church again, and I did not like the new churches she attended. My life began to move faster than I could handle. I would come in at late hours in the night. I had already started drinking occasionally when my friends and I could find someone to purchase the alcohol, which was not hard. I was doing adult things and hanging out with a much older crowd. I was not afraid of my mother because she was pregnant and she could not do anything about it.

One summer night I was out with a friend who was older than me. She asked me to go with her to her boyfriend's house. Around 10:00 p.m., I was ready to go home, but he refused to take us home. Although I had been staying out late at night, I did not want to be away from home all night. We began to walk home and walked down a street that had one way in and one way out with apartments on each side of the road. People would not drive into this area during the daytime, and we were two young girls walking through it at night.

When we got halfway down the street, there was a crowd of men on each side of the street who approached us, thinking we wanted to buy drugs. One next to me had a gun in his pocket. I had never been so scared before in my life. I just knew I was going to be killed or raped. Just then the police drove by and everyone scattered. If the police had not come, I don't know what would have happened to us that night. God's protection was with me. After that close call, I did not go anywhere with anyone in that area but continued to do what I wanted to do in other areas.

My mother had my baby brother, and things went back to the way they were. My mother worked hard to make ends meet. All her aggravation was steered towards me. We never had the mother and daughter relationship that I wanted and needed. My father was not in the picture, so I needed my mother. My best friend and her mother had a great relationship. Why couldn't I have that? By this time, I was really wild and pretty much doing everything I was big enough and bad enough to do. She didn't care. At least, that's how I felt. My mother may have really loved me then, but how would I have known? She never told me nor showed me. She only beat me and yelled at me. There was no other communication.

What I would tell a mother today? Keep the lines of communication between you and your children open. There are people that wait to take advantage of girls and boys with low self-esteem. I had no self-esteem; I didn't even care about myself. Children need to feel loved and wanted by their parents. If not, they will mistake someone being nice to them as love, when that person may be trying to manipulate them. I didn't know then how hard it was being a single parent.

I still try to invest time in my children. I am not perfect, but I refuse to let anyone else tell them what I should be telling them. My mom had a lot of added stress besides being a single parent. She was once a minister; she disobeyed God and that added to the already hard times. Therefore, I stress very strongly that you should establish a truthful relationship with God; he is all the help you will ever need. Obedience is the key. Jesus paid the price for our sins, so why not live for him? No stress should cause you to neglect your child emotionally or any other way.

"Blessed is the one who finds wisdom, and the one who gets understanding, for the gain from her is better than gain from silver and her profit better then gold."
Proverbs 3:13-14

Emotional Abuse

The National Center on Child Abuse and Neglect defines emotional abuse as: "acts or omissions by the parents or other caregivers that have caused, or could cause, serious behavioral, cognitive, emotional, or mental disorders. In some cases of emotional abuse, the acts of parents or other caregivers alone, without any harm evident in the child's behavior or condition, are sufficient to warrant child protective services (CPS) intervention. For example, the parents/caregivers may use extreme or bizarre forms of punishment, such as confinement of a child in a dark closet. Less severe acts, such as habitual scapegoating, belittling, or rejecting treatment, are often difficult to prove and, therefore, CPS may not be able to intervene without evidence of harm to the child.

The American Medical Association (AMA) describes Emotional Abuse as: "When a child is regularly threatened, yelled at, humiliated, ignored, blamed or otherwise emotionally mistreated. For example, making fun of a child, calling a child names, and always finding fault are forms of emotional abuse."

Emotional abuse is more than just verbal abuse. It is an attack on a child's emotional and social development and is a basic threat to healthy human development. Emotional abuse can take many forms such as:

1. Belittling

Belittling a child causes the child to see him or herself in the way consistent with the caregiver's words. This limits the child's potential by limiting the child's own sense of his or her potential.

2. Coldness

Children learn to interact with the world through their early interactions with their parents. If parents are warm and loving, children grow to see the world as a secure place for exploration and learning. When parents are cold to their children, they deprive them of necessary ingredients for intellectual and social development. Children who are subjected to consistent coldness grow to see the world as a cold, uninviting place and will likely have seriously impaired relationships in the future. They may also never feel confident to explore and learn.

3. Corrupting

When parents teach children to engage in antisocial behavior, the children grow up unfit for normal social experience.

4. Cruelty

Cruelty is more severe than coldness, but the results can be the same. Children need to feel safe and loved in order to explore the world around them and in order to learn to form healthy relationships. When children experience cruelty from their caretakers, the world ceases to "make sense" for them; all areas of learning are affected social, emotional, and intellectual development are hindered.

5. Extreme Inconsistency

The foundations of learning are laid in the first interactions between child and caretaker. Through consistent interactions, the child and parent shape each other, and the child learns that his or her actions have consistent consequences - this is the foundation for learning. The child also learns to trust that his or her needs will be met by others. When the caretaker is inconsistent in his or her response to the child, the child cannot learn what is expected from the start, and all areas of learning can be affected throughout the child's lifespan.

6. Harassment

Harassment has similar effects to those of belittling, but also involves a stress response. Harassment scares the child, and repeated exposure to fear can alter the child physically, lowering his/her ability to deal with other stressful situations.

7. Ignoring

Ignoring a child deprives the child of all the essential stimulation and interaction necessary for emotional, intellectual, and social development.

8. Inappropriate Control

Inappropriate control takes three forms - lack of control, over control, and inconsistent control. Lack of control puts children at risk for danger or harm to themselves and robs children of the knowledge handed down through human history. Over-control robs children of opportunities for self-assertion and self-development by preventing them from exploring the world around them. Inconsistent control can cause anxiety and confusion in children and can lead to a variety of problematic behaviors as well as impair intellectual development.

9. Isolating

Isolating a child, or cutting his/her off from normal social experiences, prevents the child from forming friendships and can lead to depression. Isolating a child seriously impairs his/her intellectual, emotional, and social development. Isolating is often accompanied by other forms of emotional abuse as well as physical abuse.

10. Rejecting

When a caretaker rejects a child, the caretaker is negating the child's self-image, showing the child that he or she has no value. Children who are rejected from the start by their caretakers develop a range of disturbed self-soothing behaviors. An infant who is rejected has almost no chance of developing into a healthy adult.

11. Terrorizing

Terrorizing, like harassment, evokes a stress response in children. Repeated evocation of the stress response alters the child physically, lowering his/her ability to fight off disease and increasing the risk for many stress-related ailments. Aside from the physical effects, a child living in terror has no opportunities to develop anything other than unhealthy and anti-social survival skills.

Emotional abuse is the core of all forms of abuse; the long-term effects of child abuse and neglect in general stem mainly from the emotional aspects of abuse. Actually, it is the psychological aspect of most abusive behaviors that defines them as abusive. Think of a child breaking his or her arm. If the arm was broken while riding a bicycle and trying to jump a ramp, the child will heal and recover psychologically, perhaps even strengthening his or her character and learning valuable life-lessons in the process by overcoming obstacles with the support of his or her caregivers and friends. If the same injury occurs because a parent twists the child's arm behind his or her back in a rage or throws the child down the stairs, the child will heal physically, but may never heal psychologically.

In thinking of sexual abuse, think of a child being examined by a doctor - doctors touch children's genitals routinely in physical examinations without damaging children in any way. But think of the same contact from a sexualized older acquaintance. It is clear that the damage from fondling the child is psychological and emotional. Now think of a child who lives with a parent who terrifies the child but who has just enough control (it's all about control) over him or herself to refrain from injuring the child physically in a way that will draw attention. That child is suffering the same devastating abuse as the children in the examples above, but often nothing can be done about it.

Despite the fact that the long-term harm from abuse is most often caused by the emotional aspects of the abuse, emotional abuse is the most difficult of the forms of abuse to substantiate and prosecute. Actual physical injury is often required before the authorities can step in and assist a child. Also, the effects of abuse are very similar to symptoms of many childhood mental and physical disorders, which make identifying emotionally abused children difficult.

Signs of Emotional Abuse and Verbal Abuse

Child's Behavior:
Appears overly compliant, passive, undemanding; Appears very anxious or depressed; Attempts suicide; Avoids doing things with other children; Behaves younger than his or her age; Finds it difficult to make friends; Is extremely aggressive, demanding, or enraged; Lags in physical, emotional, and intellectual development; Is very demanding or very obedient; Behaves very adult-like; Wets or soils the bed.

Caretaker's Behavior:
Blames or belittles child; is cold and rejecting; Withholds love; Treats siblings unequally; Seems unconcerned about child's problems.

4

Fourteen and Pregnant

My ninth grade year in middle school, I was very active in school. I was a little more focused and preparing for high school. For the most part I was excited about going to high school. I played volleyball my last year of middle school. Participating in sports in school took my mind off boys and also placed me around a different crowd. Things were good and I was on the right track.

Every evening when I got home from volleyball practice, I would walk through the housing project near our house to go to the store, occasionally stopping to talk with old friends. Every day this same guy would try to get my attention. I ignored him for weeks. Then one day he walked to the store with me and made my purchase for me. Now that was something no one had ever done. You know at that point I thought, "Oh, he must really like me." I asked him how old he was, and he replied 18, so I thought that's not bad. I gave him my number and we began to talk over the phone. He started giving me money on a regular basis, and I just took it and enjoyed the attention.

One day I found out that it was not free money. Eventually we became sexually active. Of course after becoming sexually active, I found that things that he had told me were not so true. This is when the mask came off. When we met, he told me he had a job but that was far from the truth. He sold drugs and did not have a job. In the end, after he had gotten what he wanted, the attention stopped slowly. I found out that he was much older than he told me; he was 24. He had several other girlfriends (what a surprise!), but none of this stopped me from continuing to stay involved with him.

Night after night, I sneaked him into the back door. As time passed the unexpected happened, I missed my monthly cycle. My menstrual cycle came like clockwork, always at the exact time but not this time. I waited but it never came. Finally I got up the nerve to go and find out if I was pregnant; just thinking about it made my stomach ache. What would I do? How would

I tell my mother? What would she do to me? All these questions swirled in my head. There was a safe place where teens could go for a free pregnancy test. I walked there and took a pregnancy test.

While waiting for the results, you were required to look at videos on abortions and counseling. It was a Christian-based organization, so the worker would pray with you. I can recall the lady asking what was I going to do if I was pregnant, and I did not have an answer. I could not imagine being pregnant, but I knew that I was. I could feel it in my gut. They offered adoption and discouraged abortions. After waiting for an hour, she came back with a gift and congratulated me on my pregnancy. I'm thinking, "Congratulations! My mom is really going to kill me now. "What was I going to do with a baby at 14 years old? She asked if the father would be involved, and I knew the answer to that it was "no."

I did not tell my mother; I tried to hide it. She found out when one of my close friends got mad at me and told. It was a Saturday night when she asked me about it and I could not lie. How do you hide a baby anyway? I got a whipping that night for sure; I thought the lady was trying to kill me. I cannot imagine how my mom felt; that was a very emotional night for the both of us. The next day she went to church and left me home. I knew she was embarrassed. I really became an outcast then. From the time that the pregnancy was confirmed I had no idea how to feel. Fear and pain had already become a part of my life from the beginning. My mom finally decided to just let me have the baby. My relationship with this man exposed me to things that I could not have ever imagined. Physical abuse started whenever I would interfere with him trying to be with another girl. He would start a fight and make me leave his house just to have an excuse to do what he wanted. I did not know then but that was to give him a reason to get rid of me.

The pregnancy was stressful and I was sick all the time. I started to miss days out of school. I did not want any of my teachers to know. I had another classmate who was pregnant so I did not care if other students knew. But I did not want my teachers to know because I knew they would see me differently. I remember specifically the reaction from my English teacher when my mom told the school, she treated me much differently. I was in AP classes and you were expected to have higher standards than others.

But they had to know because I was missing so many days out of school. This was my ninth grade year, and it was supposed to be one of the most memorable times of my teenage years. Well, it was memorable but not like I wanted it to be. I was invited to the prom by another classmate, but I could not go because I was pregnant. The relationship with this man did not last.

I did not hear from him throughout the entire pregnancy except when he wanted sex. My feelings and emotions were everywhere. I walked around with my head down and my self-esteem at its lowest. I spent my summer isolated from everyone. The only place I would go was to the doctor. The pregnancy was not healthy for me or the baby I was carrying.

Labor and Delivery

The summer was long; my due date was on the first day of school. I was excited about going to high school, but I still had bouts of depression and embarrassment about being pregnant. I tried to hide my feelings by building a wall to protect myself from negative comments, and I tried to fit in as much as possible. I had a doctor's appointment scheduled on the first day of school; my plans were to check in after my appointment. Unfortunately, my doctor's visit did not go as planned. There I lay on the exam table waiting to be dismissed and given my next appointment to return, but instead, another nurse came in to check my blood pressure. I was thinking, "Didn't she do that already?" Then she proceeded to ask me how I felt; I replied "Fine." Then I was told to turn on my left side. Something was wrong, but no one told me what. After rechecking my blood pressure, the nurse returned and told me to get dressed and to go to the hospital, which was next door.

I felt fine and didn't feel like I was in labor at the time. If I was in labor, I was thinking this is going to be a breeze. I was a child having a baby. Nevertheless, I was admitted to the hospital immediately. They placed me in a room and began placing intravenous fluids in my arm and still no one told me anything. After I had been there for hours, my mother came in. She was upset and asked me how I felt. I had no pain or discomfort; I felt fine. Ultimately, I became sleepy and drowsy, but I thought that was the medication. I didn't know why no one told me anything. Then I overheard the doctor tell my mother that my blood pressure was extremely elevated and that the baby was in distress.

The doctor was trying to determine the best method of delivery, and she had to decide between me and the baby. There was a possibility that either the baby or I would not live. I drifted off to sleep shortly afterwards. The next time I opened my eyes, I was awakened by the Chaplain. She was a Caucasian lady, dressed in all white; she asked if she could pray with me and I replied, "yes." I was drowsy, everything was blurry, and I was scared. After she prayed, peace came over me. I went to sleep until I was awakened and taken into surgery for a C-section.

The operating room was bright and cold; I remember fighting trying to take the oxygen mask off. Finally the medication kicked in and I was out.

The surgery went well; I thought I'm still here, thank God for that. I was very sore. I asked the nurses if I could speak to the Chaplain who prayed with me but no one knew who she was. I would love to tell you how I changed my life and became this obedient and responsible teen that did everything right. But that is far from the truth. I was discharged from the hospital after about 2-3 days post-op.

Upon arriving home, I had no idea of how to be a mother. My mind was blank. The only thing I knew was that I had my own baby. The relationship between my mother and me did not change. She would express often that I could not live in her house with a baby. Days after being discharged from the hospital I was sent back to the ER for an infection in the incision site. No one bothered to teach me how to clean the suture site. I had no idea of how to truly take care of myself in that manner. I was there another week, dealing with rude nurses and doctors with no bedside manners, but I guess they felt they could treat me that way because I was just another teen mother.

The next time I went home I was sent to live with my mother's godmother; she was one of the mothers of our home church. She adopted my brother and me into her family and tried to help raise us. I remember how she would always be sitting in her chair by the door, reading the Bible and praying all day long and speaking in her heavenly language. I used to think, "Is that all she do?" She did all she could to help me and to help take care of my son. I did not want to be helped at the time, because I was too busy trying to get home to do what I wanted to do and chase behind a no-good man. When I returned home with my mom, I received home schooling so that I could stay on track with my schooling. That did not work out well because I was not staying home. I would leave home when I knew the teacher was coming, so the homeschooling ended.

"I will never leave you nor forsake you." Deuteronomy 31:6

The time came for me to have my six-week checkup so that I could go to school. Things did not work out as planned; my results came back abnormal. I was referred to a specialist for follow-up. I was later diagnosed: I had precancerous cells in my cervix. I had no idea what he was truly saying to me, but I knew cancer did not sound good. I became scared and nervous. The doctor explained the two procedures that had to be done: first was a biopsy and afterwards was laser surgery or cryotherapy, which was freezing the tissue to minimize the possibility that it would come back later as cervical cancer.

God has spared me continuously throughout my lifetime. The time came for me to have my biopsy; I was so scared, that my body was shaking

42

like a limb on a tree. I was alone and terrified. My entire body was ice cold while lying on the table. The fear that was in me was so great that all I could do was cry out. I was crying so bad that the doctor stopped and asked if he was hurting me; he wasn't, but I was just that scared. Finally I stopped crying and began to close my eyes and pray. I heard the voice of God whisper to me these words, "Don't cry, I will take care of you now just as I did before." Immediately, I felt peace. I heard the voice of God so clearly that day, but at the time I thought that it was my imagination. The biopsy confirmed the diagnosis. The laser surgery was performed successfully without any complications. I was finally able to return to school.

I was truly blessed to receive state-funded daycare for my son while I attended school. I returned to church soon after. At church I was embarrassed and always walked around with my head down. The first Sunday at church I was called into the pastor's office. My pastor's wife sat me down and talked to me. She encouraged me to keep my head up and not be embarrassed about my situation. I tried to pretend that I was okay. I put on a mask that said I don't care what people think, but realistically, I did care. She did most of the talking. She explained that I had placed myself in an adult situation at a young age. She made me understand that I would miss out on things that the average teen would be doing. What I received was discipline with love. I appreciated it then and still do.

My first day back at school was nerve-wrecking. For the most part I felt like an outcast. I did not talk much except to the people that I had already known. I still have that habit, I only talk with people that I have become acquainted with. Otherwise, I am as quiet as a mouse. I was a good student academically, so my grades never showed the problems that I had at home. I tried not to show my low self-esteem outwardly. In an attempt to make myself feel better, I became the class clown and made everything funny. Sometimes you have to put yourself in another world to get away from the pain. So that was what I did, and I continued to suppress my unhealthy feelings.

One evening when I returned home from school, I was caught off guard when my mother and my son's grandmother told me that I should give my son away. My mother gave me an ultimatum: give my son away or find another place to live. Since I refused to give him away, I had to move out. I had nowhere to go, but that did not matter to her. The only person left for me to rely on was my son's father. When he could not come through, I would leave my son with him overnight and sleep in my mother's car without her knowledge. I remembered that her car door lock was broken, so I would sleep in the car and get up when it was time for her to go to work. I changed clothes wherever I could and went to school. I was late for school every day. Some days I had to wear the same clothes to school. I just knew I had to finish school.

Barry was abusive. Whenever I would say something he did not like or look the wrong way, he would beat me. I would go to school with black eyes and bruises. He did not have much use for me anymore. I had become too much of a responsibility. Somehow I made it through the school year, going from place to place with no one to rely on. I passed a few classes. My mom would allow me to stay the night at home when she needed me to babysit my brothers. I went from sleeping in a car to living with some distant relatives. When they no longer wanted me there, I lived with one of my friends' mother. His mom had a stroke and was in a hospital bed. He was young, so her house was where everyone would hang out. I did the best I could to take care of my son, and I went to school whenever I could.

5

Pregnant Again

In December of 1991, I decided to go to the clinic and get some birth control pills. After having my annual pap smear, I was told by the nurse that they could not give me any birth control pills. And when I asked why, she told me that I was pregnant at 16 years old with child number two. What was I going to do with another child? I was already homeless with no money and no help and a boyfriend who was abusive. I told Barry I was pregnant, but it did not make much difference to him. He arranged for me to live with one of his relatives. I lived there throughout the summer. I could not go to school but I had a warm place to lay my head and that was all that mattered. During this time I endured more and more physical abuse - yes, even pregnant. In the end, the arrangement ended because Barry stopped paying the person I was living with, so she put me out pregnant and with my son.

I had to find somewhere to go. My mom suggested that I call her god-sister. I contacted her, and she agreed to let me move in. This was the most stability I had in a long time. Barry had me on an emotional roller coaster. It seemed as if as soon as I would get past the hurt of him breaking up with me, he would come back and it would start all over again. I remember a time when he came by and asked me to stop calling him because he had someone else. The pain was unbearable. I had excruciating abdominal pain upon hearing this news. I did not eat or sleep for days. I would always vow never to return but that did not last. I had become all too familiar with those feelings of rejection, pain, and fear. Later in life it seemed as if I would just wait for rejection and pain.

Aunt Betty helped me raise my son as much as she could. She taught me how to potty train him. She threw his bottle away. I suffered from that one as he would cry all night without his bottle. She even gave me a baby shower for the new baby. I think she was happier than I was to find out that I was having a girl. Summer was over and it was time to return to school. I was excited about school. My aunt made sure I got to school every morning, and my son was in daycare again. God will definitely place people in your life for a season.

The New Baby

I was sitting at the bus stop trying to make it to school for a biology test. I knew that I was in labor, but I did not want to miss this test. Needless to say, I missed that test. The baby was not waiting. I walked around the neighborhood trying to find a ride to the hospital, and finally I did. I delivered in about an hour with no complications this time. After the delivery, my mom insisted that I come home with her this time. I had my doubts but I did. My aunt would call and ask when I was coming back. I eventually told her that I was staying with my mother. This was a big mistake. I thought maybe things had changed and she really wanted me home, but that was not the case. I figured that out later.

My 11th grade year was much better than the others. I felt as if I was accomplishing something. I almost felt normal. After returning to church, things seemed to improve; I connected with teens in the church. Barry was out of the picture for the moment. I was singing in the choir again. Then came Valentine's Day. I arrived home to a room full of flowers and candy. Guess who? Barry. I fell for his charm. The devil is very deceitful. *(Word of wisdom: If you are ever fortunate enough to get out of an unhealthy relationship do not return. Nine times out of ten that person has not changed in less than a year.)*

Barry started to go to church with me, doing all the right things to draw me in. Let me tell you, satan knows your weakness; you have to stay focused. He took me to the prom. Things were good, I thought. I had not given him an answer yet about taking him back, but I was giving him all the signals that said "yes" in the time we spent together and accepting his gifts.

Weeks after accepting him back, I began to start missing church and hanging out again. The mother of one of the teens that I was close to in church told me that Barry was going to hurt me. I thought about what she said, and shortly afterwards I began to have dreams about Barry. In the first dream, I was going to his home, and he was standing in the doorway kissing a girl when I walked up. And, yes, I knew this girl. In the second dream, the same girl in the same scenario. In the third dream, again it was the same girl and the same scenario. The dreams came three nights in a row, playing like a movie. The dreams were surreal. While on the phone one night I decided to tell him about the dreams, he laughed and said I was crazy. So I asked, "Are you sure you are not cheating?" Of course he said, "No," so we continued dating. The school year went well and I was able to catch up from the previous year. The summer was here and I attended summer school. After summer school, I would spend the day with Barry and the kids.

One evening upon arriving at Barry's house, I found him standing in the doorway kissing a girl. Yes, the very thing I saw in my dreams had come true. I became very nervous and was questioning as to how I could have dreamed this before it happened. Suddenly, I remembered another incident in which I knew something was going to happen before it did.

It was one Sunday evening after church. Everyone was walking to their cars, and there was a man walking up the street. A strange feeling came over me. I remember pulling my mother's arm, and she snatched her arm away asking, "What is wrong with you?" Abruptly, the man ran by and snatched one of the member's purse. At that moment it was as if I saw it before it happened. God gives us warnings. Since those dreams of my cheating boyfriend, every time I have been in a bad situation, I have always seen it in a dream first.

I did nothing when I saw my boyfriend kissing another girl. Although I did nothing, the incident sent me into a deep depression which I had not experienced before. I continued to date Barry but most of my time was spent at work. My mom liked the fact that I was working now. But during this time Barry and I went through some changes. You see I no longer needed his money, and that took away some of his control. So the relationship was off and on. The downside of having a job was missing church.

The devil had me just where he wanted me. I was no longer going to church consistently and my focus was elsewhere. It felt like something wasn't right. Barry no longer wanted to babysit while I worked, so I got a second job at Burger King to pay for childcare. And that is when I started working two jobs at the age of 17. My mom was upset that I was working and missing church.

On the other hand, I was finally able to take care of myself and my children. I was not satisfied with being on food stamps and welfare. I wanted my children to have a good future. The end of summer was soon approaching. I had caught up on all my classes and was going to graduate on time.

Soon it became difficult to live with my mom so I decided to move. There were some new apartments being built near my neighborhood so I saved the money for the deposit. Ironically I knew the owner. His wife was my Spanish teacher, which made the application process easy. But when it was time to move, I changed my mind and decided to tough things out with my mother.

6
My 12th Grade Year

I made it to the 12th grade, almost time to graduate. I started out doing well. I continued to work at the Waffle House, but I had to quit my second job at Burger King. Working a job and going to school was challenging. By the end of the first semester, I was tired and overwhelmed. I was not doing well in my classes. I knew that I had to work to keep from depending on anyone. I remember sitting in my English class taking my mid-terms and trying to decide what to do. I decided within that hour that I would quit school and get my GED. In my eyes, I needed to support myself and my kids. Moreover, my mother did not care whether I finished or not, and I eventually didn't care either.

I have learned that even when no one else cares about your future, you still have to care about yourself. In reality, I did not care much about myself, but I began to push myself for the children. I never wanted them to suffer.

I left school that day and went to a nearby technical college and took the test for my GED. I passed and waited to enroll in college with my other classmates at the end of the school year. So far every significant milestone I should have experienced growing up I had missed. Now I had all this extra time on my hands.

Too Much Idle Time

Most of my time was spent working and spending time around my children's fathers' family. It was a while before my mother noticed that I was not going to school. I worked as much as I could. By the time my daughter was a year old, I was pregnant again. This time I knew that I could not have another baby. I had a friend at work who was like a big sister, always looking out for me. She was like that big sister that I never had. She talked me into having an abortion. She gave me a lecture on how I was too young to have so many children; I would have been seventeen with three children. She was aware of my mother and our relationship. Everything she was saying to me was true; I could not afford to have another baby. She made me save every dime until I had the money for an abortion. She would hold the money so that I would not spend it. The day of my appointment came. She dropped me off at the clinic. In front of the building were people with their signs protesting against abortions. I was hoping no one bombed the place while I was there.

There is a process before having the abortion. You are required to go through counseling first. I sat there listening to all the other women who were trying to make me feel better about what I was doing. There were people there who were married; I did not understand why a married couple would have to abort a baby. One lady told me that it was her seventh abortion. Yes, I was mentally judging them. I sat there in amazement. It is amazing the things a teen can do without adult consent these days.

Well, it was my turn. I was not put to sleep because I could only afford the gas for sedation. After dressing into the hospital gown I lay on the table. I heard the machine turn on; it sounded like a vacuum. It felt as if the doctor was taking out my insides. It was over in less than 15 minutes. A life gone in 15 minutes.

My friend picked me up. I was silent the entire way home. They gave me pain pills, but I wanted to die. I knew what I did was wrong and I could not see myself living with it. When my mom came home that evening I was sleeping. She came in yelling because I was apparently supposed to pick my brother up from school. When she asked where I was all day, I broke down and told her. She told me that I needed to get my life together and then she told me that I would not become anything. I did not want to hear this; I felt bad enough. I had just killed a baby.

I repented over and over again, but I always felt condemned. I knew who God was, but I was lost in complete darkness. I tried other relationships whenever Barry and I broke up, but relationships did nothing for me; I was only digging myself into a bigger hole. I was completely out of church, and no one at the church was trying to reach me. Time went on and I continued to work and do my own thing. I spent my time in the clubs at night when I was not at work.

My mother had been saying she wanted me to leave her house. After listening to her for so long, I just tuned her out. One evening when I got off work, she was moving. She left me and my kids in the house we were living in.

Shortly afterwards, I found out that the house did not pass inspection and was considered unlivable because of the space heaters. My mother never told me that. She left me with bills, and I had no idea how to handle things. I did the best that I could. Friends helped me to pay the bills. She did leave us with a bed. I really had to depend on Barry.

I needed more money to make it, and since Barry sold drugs, I tried to do the same thing. That did not last long. I was too scared, and I felt sorry for the people that were on drugs. The last bag of crack I had, I gave it away. I just could not do it. I could not handle the guilt.

7
Another Baby

At this time Barry and I was off and on, nothing serious. I did not have time for him anymore. Now the drama begins. You remember I told you earlier that I liked to club, well I was a heavy drinker, too. One night while out with some friends I ran into a mutual friend of Barry and me. The both of us had a little too much to drink and ended up at a hotel. We agreed not to ever mention it. A month later I was pregnant, and I could not remember if we used protection. I called him, and he told me that he used protection. I was relieved.

The problem came when I decided to confide in a so called friend and the news spread like wildfire. I was worried about Barry finding out, and if by chance he did, I was going to deny it. Unfortunately, the news came directly from me, because Barry walked in while I was on the phone with another friend, telling her about the affair. What's in the dark always comes to light! For the first time I saw him cry; this friend was someone he called his cousin. I could not believe he was crying. I think he was crying only because he was embarrassed. I justified my action by bringing up all the times he had cheated, even with my relatives. He had slept with several of my friends and cousins.

In the midst of the pregnancy, I had to listen to everyone talking about me. I was called everything but a child of God. I assured Barry that the baby was his. He forgave me. The pregnancy went on, but I became mean and hateful. At least, that's what my mom said, and soon I began to fit that description towards people who I believed did not care about me. If I felt as if you meant me no good, then that is how I treated you. So I guess you can say I treated people the way they treated me. That did not make it right.

A Change Was Coming, But Not A Good Change

Barry and I moved in together and tried to function as a couple. Things began to change; I finally realized that this was not the person I wanted to spend the rest of my life with. After all the years of lying and cheating, I started to look for reasons to break up with him. There were times when I would just throw his clothes out the house to give him a reason to leave. I remember one night I threw his clothes out the window and rolled his TV down the stairs.

After years of abuse, I began fighting back, we fought often. I remember one night he was stopped by the police and taken to jail. He had drugs on him. His family called me, expecting me to get him out. Oh, no, not me! I don't know who bailed him out that night but I refused to do it. The entire family was mad at me. I just did not care anymore. He could have stayed there until eternity, and I would not have cared. This man had fathered so many children during the time we were together until I just said forget it. My best friend Tamara would always tell me, "Shanta, you and Barry are like oil and water - y'all don't mix." Finally, I started to see that after all those years.

The Baby Is Coming

On Christmas Eve I started having contractions but tried my best to make it to the end of my work shift. I didn't make it. Since Barry still had some of his old ways, I could not find him to pick me up from work. I had to get the cook that night to take me home. To my surprise, Barry was home that night sleeping. I was in a lot of pain, but I was not ready to go to the hospital. I knew they would just have me to lie in bed in pain and wait until time to deliver, and I did not want to do that. Barry and I argued back and forth about going to the hospital. Eventually I did go and I delivered at 6:00 a.m. Christmas morning of 1995. I remember the nurse asking me, "What are you going to name the baby?" The doctor responded, "I think her name is going to be Jesus, because that is what she yelled the entire time." It's amazing how we know God when we need him. As time went on, I was discharged from the hospital with my third child at the age of 19.

One Month Post-Partum & Pregnant Again

One month after my six week checkup, I was pregnant again. I definitely could not have this baby. I had already mentally decided that I did not want to spend the rest of my life with this man, so I had another abortion. I prayed and made a vow to God that I would not have another after this one. Barry did not want me to do it, but I did not want another child with him. I had a cousin who told me, "Every baby you kill you are going to have anyway." I think she was right.

I went to another clinic; the one I used before was closed. I sat through the group counseling. I listened to this woman attempt to dispel all the myths about abortions. She did not do a good job at making me feel better. She told us that she had had an abortion ten years ago and now look at her; she was dry and pale as a ghost that was my counseling. I went through with it. I used birth control after that. I got to the point in my life where I felt like I just wanted to start over. I wanted a change, but I did not know how to get it.

I decided to move to an entirely different environment, away from Barry and his family. I remember the day I was approved for section 8. I moved everything in one day. I knew that he would not move away from his family. That was out of his comfort zone.

8
Trying To Make A Change

A brand new start! At least that is what I thought it would be. I found out over time that changing the environment does not help if you do not change. The problem was I wanted a change, but I was doing it the wrong way. I didn't think about going back to church or rededicating my life to Christ. The devil had become my father instead of God. I only prayed when I needed something or if I was in trouble.

When I look back over my life, I see that God never let me go. The problem was I let him go. In the Book of Isaiah, chapter 9, the prophet talks about Gods anger against his chosen people, but there was a phrase that is repeated several times that got my attention: "But his hand is stretched out still." In the midst of our mess, God never removes his hand. He does allow certain things to happen, but he does not leave us, we leave him.

I moved away from Barry and started seeing other people. A relationship was not what I needed then, but I didn't know that. I needed to heal, but I did not see that. Barry was out of the picture for a while until one day he called and said that he needed somewhere to live. He and his mother had had a fight, and she put him out. I told him that he could stay as long as he understood that we were not in a relationship. That was a joke. He had a problem whenever anyone called me or if I went out somewhere. It was a bad decision to let him move in!

The guy I was involved with at the time was a friend's cousin. One night my new friend and I were going to the Fair. We were sitting in his driveway talking, and out of nowhere Barry came and parked behind my car. He swung the door open, jumped out of the car and began banging on the car window. I knew what was going to happen, so I told Sean not to open the door. He was scared so he opened the door anyway. Barry pulled him out the car. He took over the driver seat and drove off, speeding with the doors open.

We had had fights before, but this time I saw something different in his face. We were arguing and fighting while he was driving.

Can you believe he did all of this and yet he was with another girl? He left her in the other car that he had driven to follow me. He kept yelling, "I am going to kill you!" We were yelling and fighting while he was driving. The arguing stopped when he pulled into a wooded area surrounded by trees. I could see an apartment complex afar off but no one was around. That night he literally tried to beat me to death. Out of rage he picked up a glass beer bottle that was on the ground, and just as he lifted his hand to hit me in the head with it, a man yelled out threatening to call the police. At that moment I had given up, and I knew I was going to die that night. He took off running on foot and I drove myself to the ER. I was checked out, the police did a report, and Barry was arrested. This incident forced me to leave Barry alone completely.

Another Relationship Gone Badly

Since I was no longer in a relationship at that time, I worked non-stop. I spent very little time with my children. I could not manage my money and was always behind on my bills. I struggled and never had time to hang out anymore. I worked two jobs to make ends meet. I was on section 8 and still struggled with my rent of only sixty dollars. I had no desire to seek God; I was lost in all my sin. I did not have any reliable help, so I would have to leave my children unattended to work. I was more focused on buying my children all the name brand clothes and shoes, but I wasn't being a mother. I became lonely after a while and started talking to an old classmate who lived across the street from me at that time. I had no goals, no vision, no dream and priorities; what were those? Barry was out of the picture, but he would call and leave messages that he hated me and that he was not going to do anything for the children.

After talking to my new friend for a month, it grew into a relationship. His name was Jamal; he did not have any children, so he would babysit and cook for the children while I worked. He wanted a more serious relationship than I did and suggested moving in together almost immediately. I wasn't sure about that, but I started looking at the supposedly financial benefits of the move. I thought that I would be able to pay my bills and have money left over. By moving in with him, I could do a lot of things; at least that is what I thought. Shacking did not end my problems but instead compounded them. I did not have the feelings or the intentions that Jamal had. I had just gotten out of a seven-year-long, abusive relationship. Jamal wanted a future together and to get married, but I did not. I knew his intentions, but mine were selfish intentions. I didn't love this man.

The move was very controversial; his mom did not want him with someone with three children. I remember her asking him, "What are you going to do with a girl with three children?" But we moved in together anyway. The initial problem was the male friends I had. He wanted me to get rid of my friends, and I did not want to. I limited my friends to just calling my cell phone. I remember the weekend I went out of town with a friend and stayed overnight. Jamal did not speak to me for weeks. I eventually apologized and stopped hanging out shortly afterwards. I did not even have any consideration for my children then. I thought just taking care of them financially showed my love. Now don't get me wrong I truly loved my children, but I did not know how to be a mother.

Jamal was a good person initially, he watched the kids while I worked. He would give me his check every payday to pay bills and keep the rest. Instead of doing things the right way, I took advantage and became full of arrogance. He wasn't abusive initially. I guess you're wondering what went wrong. Jamal had some issues that came out later. He had very low self-esteem, and over time he wanted attention that I was not giving him. He needed me to validate him. He became very controlling. I could not even speak to old male classmates that I saw in passing without him getting mad. He would get mad and say that I spent more time at work than at home. That was true. I grew accustomed to working two jobs.

After growing tired of working so much, I decided to go back to school. I had started Nursing School at Auburn University in Montgomery but dropped out. So I reenrolled into a technical college to become a Licensed Practical Nurse with plans of going back later for my RN. I needed more income so that I could be home more. In fact, what I needed was to change everything that was wrong in my life and set priorities and goals. Jamal was spending more time with the children than I was. He helped them with their homework and attended school functions. Somewhere I became selfish without knowing it.

In the fall of 1996, I started school at Trenholm State Technical College. In the initial orientation they taught about time management. The instructors warned that any and every thing that could go wrong would, while we were trying to complete the program. They gave us testimonials of their past experiences. They told us that we would not be able to work at all because we had to learn a large amount of information in less than two years. They were right about things going wrong. Jamal became very jealous and became my biggest obstacle in completing school. It was not easy. I continued to work two jobs, and I would be up late at night doing homework. I fell asleep in class often. Towards the end of the program I found out I was pregnant. My delivery date was during mid-terms. Ironically I went in labor the Friday before the week of spring break. I had my fourth child on March 28, 1998. I had to rest that week and I returned to school after that week. I had to deal with Jamal's arguing.

Nursing school was stressful after having a baby and returning to school one week postpartum and work three weeks later. I was stressed and depressed. We argued constantly about the lack of time we were spending together. He was not getting any attention. He wanted to be married and I did not. I never had those kinds of feelings for him. I knew that I was not ready for marriage.

9
Drama

One weekend Jamal's mother had a cook-out. We all sat around joking and laughing, and I started to make fun of the fact that he was not getting any sex from me. When we returned home, we had a fight that became physical. This was the first time of many that he hit me. I knew I was stuck. I had given up my apartment, and I could not live with my mother. I stayed with a hidden agenda to move after I completed school. I missed a final exam at school, so I had to take my business to school: I had to let them know what happened so that I could take my test.

Jamal lost his job and had a hard time finding another one, so I had to deal with the backlash from that. He would just sit around, smoking marijuana and talking down about himself. I was almost finished with the nursing program. I had no idea then but now I know that the grace of God was how I made it. I had a 3.0 GPA. Even I did not understand how. Finally I completed the program. I completed Licensed Practical Nurse school, successfully working two jobs when I was told that I would not be able to work at all. God brought me through.

Everything that I was warned about in the beginning did happen. There were numerous unforeseen obstacles, but God brought me through. It was a relief to be finished with the program, but it was also heartbreaking because our class had turned into family for me. We had a capping ceremony and my mom attended. It was a very special night. I sat for state boards and passed on the first try.

While I was waiting to take boards, I had more time on my hand so I continued to work two jobs and sometimes three jobs. That did not last but six months. I started to become friends with other guys and involve myself in relationships outside of my current relationship. I no longer wanted to be with Jamal, but I had to wait until I saved some money to move. We did not argue as much, but I was no longer interested in trying to be in a relationship with him. I was headed in the wrong direction. A danger zone!

The Infidelity

I met guys at work who treated me better than Jamal, so I started cheating. I had already decided that I did not want to be with him anyway, so I used that to justify what I did to make me feel better. It was easy; at the time he thought I was perfect and would not do anything wrong. I normally would not but I was vengeful and still angry about him hitting me and about everything else in my life. Looking back, I remember when I said that I would never cheat on anyone or marry the wrong person, but everything that I said I would never do, I did.

After living a lie for a while, I decided to move out. Jamal thought that I was moving because of him, but the truth was that I could no longer live there, knowing that I was seeing other people. I saw myself treating him almost like I had been treated in the past by Barry. I moved out with the kids to a lodge. In all this, I did not consider what I was putting my children through. All I knew was to provide material things, which was to me being a mother.

Little did I know that buying them things was not showing love or affection; I was damaging them emotionally. Jamal would call often, asking me to come back, but I would never go. I was happy doing my own thing. I was involved with someone else. We finally had a talk one day. His excuse for being so possessive was because he felt that when I finished school, I was going to leave him. He was right, but I did not admit that to him.

After a month of being in a relationship with my new beau, Marcus, I found out that I was pregnant. This would be baby number five; I was 24 years old at this time. Shortly after finding out that I was pregnant, Marcus told me that he just wanted to be friends. I was devastated. I had no idea what to do. I really did not know much about him except that he was from Florida and was in Alabama, going to school. He did everything he could to avoid me and the pregnancy.

I decided that I would have another abortion, but I did not have the money to do so. I was going to abandon my promise to never have another abortion. Since Jamal was still asking me to come back, I decided to go back with him. I told him I was pregnant, but I did not tell him that the baby was not his. Little did I know that, while he was begging me, he had already moved on. This just became one big mess. Since we were going to try to work things out, I thought it would be best to be honest with him about everything. A co-worker warned me not to do it but I did. I told him about all the times I had cheated on him. He was hysterical. His mother was even hurt; we had become very close.

Jamal asked the million-dollar question, "Is the baby you are pregnant with mine?" I responded, "I do not know," but I really did know that it wasn't. I misled him throughout half of the pregnancy. He told me, "Since we were being honest, I have to tell you something; I have a baby on the way." I actually had the nerve to be mad. I became jealous because I knew that my baby wasn't his, and the father did not want to have anything to do with me or the baby. I decided to stay in the relationship and deal with this other girl and her pregnancy. I thought this was actually my way out of the mess, but instead I dived in deeper. Big mistake! That only caused confusion.

Jamal would go back and forth between me and his girlfriend. He would be with me one night and with her the next. One night, I was finally fed up with his cheating and decided to repay him for lying to me. I called his sister and found out where his girlfriend lived. I told his sister that I was on my way to pick her up so she could go with me. Before heading out, I grabbed Jamal's clothes and threw them in the trunk. When I arrived at his girlfriend's house, I took his clothes, placed them next to her car, and set them on fire. His sister slashed all the car's tires. This was supposed to take away the pain and make me feel better, but it did not. I felt so bad after doing this that I went back to where I was living and cried.

A few hours later, Jamal's sister called and said that the police had come to her house and questioned her about the clothes. I learned that I had placed the burning clothes too close to the car, and it ignited the car. It appeared to be intentional since the tires were slashed. I was already feeling guilty about what I had done, and now I was looking at going to jail for arson. I did not know what to do. After talking with his sister, we decided to stick with our story which was we did not do it. I could not understand why the police were so sure we had done it. They had an eye witness who knew my car and would testify. Jamal's sister convinced me that they would not be able to prove it, so I avoided the police for weeks.

Then one day I realized that I could not hide any more, and I went to the Fire Department. With my four children and pregnant with number five, I spoke with the chief; he explained my rights. I finally told the truth and requested that Jamal's sister's name be concealed; I would take all the blame. At that time I was told that Jamal's girlfriend wanted me to pay damages, and then I would not be charged. When she was asked to confirm this, she instead said she wanted charges to be brought against me. I lived, waiting for the moment that I would be picked up and taken to jail. I continued to maintain an off and on relationship with Jamal just as it was before with him going back and forth between the both of us. This girl and I had a countless number of arguments. There was a restraining order against me, and she harassed me continuously, reminding me that I was going to jail. As time passed, I waited for a court date.

On December 25, 1999, I had my fifth child at the age of 24. Months had passed, and I had forgotten about the incident with the car. I thought maybe she had changed her mind about the charges. Time went on. She had her baby in February. At the time, Jamal and I were so-called living together. He called me at work, telling me that she was in labor. He asked if I would mind if he went to the hospital. I knew it would have been wrong to say no, so I said, "Sure go ahead." I was hurting so bad that night. It felt as if my heart was literally hurting.

I sat at work waiting for him to call with an update but he never did. When I got off from work, I sat up waiting for a call; he was not answering his phone. I made the bold move to go up to the hospital. He met me at the elevator and told me that the girl was having a hard time delivering and that the baby was in distress. I left feeling bad.

The next day Jamal did not come home or call, so I went to the hospital again. I met the baby's grandmother, and then the truth came out. Everything he had told me was a lie; there was nothing wrong with her or the baby. All of it was a lie, and he had been with her the entire time. He took her to doctors' appointments without my knowledge. I felt stupid, especially since he was using my mother's car that I had begged her to let him use to get around in. After leaving the hospital, I packed all of his things and sat them on the porch. When he came home, he cried, pleaded, and begged to stay, but I could no longer do this. Over time I revealed to him that my son was not his.

Some time had passed, and there was no word from the police. Then, on March 1, 2000, as I arrived at work, I was approached by the director of nursing who told me that the police were at the front of the building, asking for me. She asked if I wanted to leave out the back door, but I had to face this and not run. The police read me my rights, while I stood there crying and trembling. They asked me where my kids were, and I told them. They were going to have the children picked up by child protective services. While I was standing there crying, the administrator of the nursing home spoke with the police who agreed to allow me three days to turn myself in. They assured me that if I did not turn myself in, I would be arrested and taken to jail for more than my current charge. At that time I was being charged with a felony.

After three days I turned myself in, and Jamal's mother paid my bail. My mother and aunt went with me. I was back in court on March 23, 2000, to make a plea. Initially, I pleaded not guilty because I did not want to lose my nursing license. Eventually, they made a deal to drop the charge to a misdemeanor, which allowed me to still work as a nurse and maybe not affect my license. On March 27, 2000, I went for my hearing. I was so embarrassed, standing there, listening to Jamal's girlfriend portray me as this jealous ex-girlfriend in a jealous rage. Harming her car was never my intentions, but I admitted to trying to hurt him.

On the eve of my sentencing two months later, I was at work when one of my co-workers asked to pray with me. She prayed with me and told me, "Shanta, your future does not depend on the person that is accusing you and not even the judge, but it is up to God."

The next morning while waiting in the courtroom for my case to be called, I sat next to a man who was reading the Bible. The Bible appeared to be two centuries old. He began to read scriptures aloud to me. I was trying to ignore him, but I heard every word. When my case was called, I walked slowly to the front of the courtroom. As the judge stated the charges, he asked if I understood the charges brought against me, and I said "Yes." I was sentenced to one year in prison suspended to two years' probation, anger management classes, and restitution for the car. When the judge asked how much I could pay monthly towards my restitution, I told her $50 a month. The judge approved the amount. Immediately a gasp from the plaintiff could be heard. The plaintiff was disappointed because I did not go to jail and did not have to pay a large lump sum of money.

The anger management classes were very beneficial. I learned to take responsibility for my actions. I also learned that although I had a passive personality, it was just as dangerous as being aggressive. People who are passive hold their feelings in, until one day something triggers their emotions, and they explode, letting out years of anger and rage. I had a lot of anger and rage within me. I began to change my attitude. I cannot give the classes all the credit for my change. God's grace was at work. I should have been fired from my job, but I wasn't. I could have been taken to jail with no way to bond out, and my kids would be in foster care. I could have been charged with a felony, lost my nursing license, and put in prison for a year. I am so glad that God said, "No!" I realize I jeopardized my freedom, my kids, and my career, trying to get revenge and hurt someone. We could even have killed someone, but thank God that did not happen.

Over time, I began to get involved with my son's biological father Marcus. One day he decided to come and see the baby. He acted like a daddy for a while. I became involved again with Marcus, and within a month I was pregnant with baby number six. He was not very happy and I wasn't either. That was the last thing I needed. I did everything I could to abort the pregnancy with no success. I eventually went to the doctor and my pregnancy was confirmed. A week later I was bleeding and went for an evaluation and discovered that I had a miscarriage. I was relieved and depressed. I felt guilty for not wanting the baby. I began taking pain medication that the doctor had given me just to go to sleep at night. I could not find any peace. To make matters worse, Marcus left town without saying anything. More Pain. What was I going to tell my son about his father?

We never consider the children when we go from man to man or relationship to relationship. Every decision you make affects your child. By the time my son was a year old, his father came back into the picture. You see Marcus had to go home and explain to his mother, father, and girlfriend that he had a baby in Alabama. After all this drama, we tried the relationship thing again, and again I ended up pregnant.

This time the baby was fine, but after finding out about the pregnancy, he decided that the relationship was not going to work out. I was stuck again alone and about to be evicted from my apartment. I was too busy with relationships to manage my finances and pay my bills on time. But in the midst of all this, I was reported for leaving my children home alone while I worked. I could not afford a babysitter, so I would leave them home alone and call to check on them every hour. Happily, I did not get in any more trouble than that but I still did not learn my lesson.

A month later I was evicted from my apartment with five children and one on the way. Homeless again. We moved from hotel to hotel. I worked a lot so I would leave my children with friends. I started working the night shift at the hospital. That way I would not have to worry about having anywhere to sleep and my children would stay with a co-worker at night. I slept in my car when I was not working. As long as my kids had somewhere to lay their heads, I was fine.

After some time, God blessed us with another place to live. Things were fine, and I worked like crazy: over 160 hours every two weeks. I was sent home one day because I had been at work for 24 hours. Crazy-huh! I gave birth to my sixth child on January 29, 2002, about a year and a half after my previous pregnancy. Jamal did not want much to do with the baby in the beginning. We did establish a relationship to the point that he would call to check on the children. Things were going fine, I stayed clear of any relationships, but my biggest problem was working too much.

10
Almost Home

One day I was called at work to come home. Child Protective Services were at my apartment. Someone had called then and reported that my children were being left unattended which they were; I could not afford a babysitter. The detectives were called, and I was arrested in front of my children. I rode in the car with the social worker and listened as she talked to me as if I were nothing. I did everything that I could to provide for my children with no help from anyone. I wasn't receiving any government benefits; therefore, I felt they had no right to come in and take my children. They called all the kids' fathers to place the children without using foster care. My oldest three children had the same father, and so they went to stay with his mother. My fourth child was able to go with her father, but my two youngest boys had nowhere to go since their father was in Florida and could not help. They were placed in temporary foster care; my baby was only three months old at the time.

While they were gone, I was supposed to come up with a plan to solve my babysitting problems. I did not have a plan, I had no help, and my mother refused to take any of my children. She thought foster care was a good idea. I was hurt, I felt like my children were all I had. Their fathers were not reliable; they did not even pay child support. Child Protective Services did not help either; they created more problems instead of helping solve them. A social worker who has no children and only has a dog at home cannot tell you how to provide for and raise six children with no family support or support from fathers!

The only thing they can do is tell you what they were taught to get their degree in that area. In the end, they ended up providing child care, and I changed shifts at work. I was able to piece myself together by the grace of God. I finally got all my children back, and the courts gave me a warning and required the state to help me.

I still did not learn my lesson. I soon got involved with someone else, Robert, after getting my children back. A month later, you guessed it, I was pregnant again with baby number seven at the age of 27. I became even more depressed. I did not really know this man. And after he found out I was pregnant, things were just like the previous father. I went through this pregnancy alone. When I delivered, he was there, and we remained together following the birth of my baby. He decided that he wanted to become serious. He was only 20 years old. We were able to maintain a relationship for a while. I moved to a better apartment and we moved in together. This was it for me. I could not live with anyone else without being married, so we decided to get married.

Now we had not known each other but for a year if that long. We tried to make the relationship work. I wanted to do the right thing, but it was the wrong time and the wrong person. I said yes to marriage but something was not right. I decided to pray and ask God about it; yes, I still knew God even though I was living a sinful life. I learned a long time ago that if you want to know if someone is right for you, just ask God and he will reveal it, so I prayed and asked God to show me anything that I did not know about him. The next day when I got off work, a girl called and asked for him. When I told her who I was, she said that she had no idea he had a girlfriend or a baby for that matter. We fought over the phone.

The next day I found a baby picture lying around the house, and the baby in the picture was identical to his baby picture. My stomach started to hurt really badly. That's when you know the truth because you feel it in your gut. I let that go and the day after that, some girl called and said that she needed pampers for her baby. Mind you, I thought my daughter was his first child. Well, he had lied and said that he did not have a baby. When I got to work that day, I called his father and asked him. He said, "Yes, he has a daughter." I was devastated. I decided to deal with it and move on any way.

The next day I was talking with Robert's mother about it, and her reply was, "Which baby?" I said, "There's another one?" She said, "He has two and your daughter is number three." I was speechless! God answered my prayers but guess what, I ignored them. I felt like I had to marry him. I had seven children, what else was I going to do? Every time we tried to go to the courthouse to get married, things came up. We moved together into a home that belonged to his father. After moving in together, I still had my doubts but I was leaning towards marriage. I asked my friends for advice. My closest friends said, "Do not marry him." I was not satisfied with that answer, so I asked a co-worker that I had befriended since she had known Robert longer than I, and she said, "Girl, go ahead he is nice."

Let me tell you that those words were not enough to hold a marriage together. First of all, I knew it was not right; otherwise, why had I prayed about it first but I could no longer handle having so many children and not being married, so out of nowhere I left work on my lunch break and got married. After that day my life was a blur, which is when I really stepped completely out of God's will and became blind to all truth. The marriage lasted a maximum of two months.

After marriage I asked my mom to help him get a job with her, and she did. Over time something was not right; I felt like he was being unfaithful but I just brushed if off. I thought that he would not do anything working with my mother; that was what I told myself. I was wrong, he was sending roses to someone at the job. My mother knew and said that she did not tell me because she knew I would not believe her. That really hurt.

Things really got out of hand then; to get revenge I started a relationship as well. I would stay out all night sometimes. I did not care anymore. I was fornicating and committing adultery. We were fighting all the time. Another unhealthy relationship. And guess what? The co-worker that I got advice from was not reliable; her husband was abusing her and on drugs. Be careful who you take advice from.

Since I did not heed God's warnings, he allowed me to do what I wanted to do. Subsequently, I had to move because Robert's father no longer wanted us in his house. We had been in so many fights and called the police so many times. It was not until I moved out of that house that things began to change. I managed to find another rental home to move into. Initially, I continued to live a sinful life. I did not pray or seek God. I had not been to church in years. After moving out, I continued to do whatever I wanted to do, without God in my life.

At times we tried to work on the marriage, but it never worked, we could not see eye to eye. I resumed working more than 160 hours every two weeks to make ends meet, living from paycheck to paycheck. At that time I was working at a nursing home. One morning I got up for work, and my car was gone. I was astounded; I was so frustrated, I did not know what to do. I had to rely on other people and sometimes ride the bus. I just did not know what was going on.

One night while at work, I was sitting out on the Gazebo, just thinking. One of my co-workers came out, her name was Anne. We used to laugh at her because she appeared to be a little eccentric. Everyone thought she was crazy, but I knew there was something special about her. She would always tell people her testimony. She came out and asked if she could pray with me.

I sort of smirked and laughed to myself thinking, "I don't need you to pray with me; I know God." I was so blind.

Prior to her praying for me, she told me that I had a calling on my life and that the devil was going to bring my past up to hurt me, but she rebuked him right then, The smirk I had went away. You see no one on my job knew anything about my past. She told me things only God knew. At that point I was so embarrassed, because I knew I should never have lived the way I was living. I had been saved since I was eight and speaking in tongues since I was fifteen. None of that mattered because I was lost in the world. My life had given people the impression that I did not know God, when I did.

Almost immediately after our prayer, my friend's boyfriend called and said that he saw my car parked at a club. We called the police and she took me to get my car. Now this is when God really showed himself. The supervisor who was working that night disliked me and had made it known, saying, "Everyone listens to you and looks up to you. You have more influence over people than me." I never knew that but that same supervisor allowed me to leave and get my car. Then when I returned, she offered to pay to have the locks on the car changed and gave me gas money. I was speechless.

It is true, God will make your enemies your footstool. This supervisor had spent most of her time trying to get me fired. I decided at that time to get myself together. I began going to church with Anne. The first time I went to her church, it was so different from my home church. The church was predominately Caucasian and so peaceful and quiet. I, on the other hand, had been raised in a Holiness church with the drums, keyboard, and guitar and much louder worship. This experience was so different, but the worship was so genuine, and I still felt the presence of God. That Sunday, I rededicated my life to Christ. I ended all relationships but my friendship with Jamal. At times I tried to fix my marriage but it did not work. I began to read the Bible every night. I started by reading the book of John seven times. When my children would go to school, I would pray nonstop for hours. My life began to change instantly. I had established a true relationship with God and it had happened so fast. He started to talk to me and show me things. This was when I began to see everything that God had done for me. I had a love so deep in my heart for Jesus that nothing could hinder it. I did not care if I was broke or on the street. I told God that I would serve him no matter what. The devil tried to hinder me several times, but his attempts failed.

After getting my car back, I decided to get another job because even after the things the supervisor did for me, she was still trying to get me fired. One day she accused me of yelling at a resident, and that was the last straw

I had to go. I turned in my resignation and told the administrator why. The administrator called me into her office and told me how she hated to see me leave, but she understood. She guaranteed me that my last two weeks on the job would be peaceful without any problems, and she made it known to everyone. I left and began working at another nursing home with a pay increase.

Marcus, the father of my two youngest boy's, and I had maintained a friendly relationship throughout all of this. I discussed with him my desire to move. I wanted to move to the North, but he suggested Atlanta where he was located so that he could be close to the boys. I debated on what I should do. If I was going to move, I needed another car, so I said, "Lord, if it is meant for me to leave, then you will provide me with a new car." The car I had at the time was not running well and I did not have the credit required to get another one as my credit rating was in the pits. Getting a new car was the only way I could move, so one day I decided to go look for one. I went to several "buy here, pay here" and they could not help me. A car dealer manager suggested that I go to a new car dealership. I left there discouraged, thinking there is no way I can get a new car. He had given me the name of a sales person to speak with.

That day after getting to work, I began telling one of my co-workers about my day and about what happened when I tried to get a car. I told her what the dealership suggested; she encouraged me to go, so I said it won't hurt to try. That following morning I went to a dealership. The salesperson that was recommended just happened to be a born-again believer who shared with me a miraculous testimony about his life. I went there to get a 1999 Honda Accord. I waited and waited. After sitting there for eight hours, I began to pray, and the only scripture that came to mind was Philippians 4:6, which says, "Be anxious for nothing but in everything by prayer and supplication with thanksgiving make your requests be made known unto God."

When the salesman came back he said, "Mrs. Mitchell, I have some bad news and some good news which do you want first?" I replied, "The bad." The bad news was that he could not get me in the Honda. I started to wonder what in the world the good news is. He asked, "What would you do if I got you in a new car?" I said, "I would shout all over this place," and he said, "Start shouting." And just in case you missed the blessing, my credit was so bad I could not get a car from a "buy here, pay here," but God blessed me with a brand new car with no miles and a full tank of gas. The same ten dollars I had when I got there was the same ten dollars I left there with. God showed himself as my provider that day.

71

Now that I had decided to live for Christ, the devil really started to mess with me. I started to have problems with people on my job. One evening while working, I was called by the police department saying that I needed to come home. I already knew what was going to happen. I began to pray at that point, I refused to worry. When I arrived home I was expecting to go to jail, but instead God moved like always, and I was given a warning and placed under supervision by the Department of Children Services. I never tried to justify what I did but I always felt that I did what I had to do to survive.

The social worker offered help but also placed obstacles in my path as well. I told him since I could not seem to get any help, I would quit my job and get welfare. He said, "No, we do not want you to do that." At that point, I decided that I needed a bigger change for me and my children. I decided to move to Atlanta. My biggest obstacle would be getting an apartment with bad credit. Marcus mailed me the application. I completed it and after about a week it was approved. I could not believe it. God had made it possible. Not only was the apartment approved but the first month was free. I paid nothing except for a deposit.

My other children's fathers were mad but I did not care. People said that I would not make it, but I am still standing. I maintained my relationship with God and it grew stronger. I moved all my things in about two days. Jamal lived in the same apartment complex and helped with the children. He took them to church on Sundays because I was still trying to work out my notice at my job in Montgomery. After working out my notice, I began looking for a job in Atlanta. We were doing much better. Before I got a job, I was home daily and able to see the children off to school and be at home when they returned. I had never been able to do that before. It is amazing how God works things out when you are in his will. I had no problem paying my rent, utilities, or car payment with no job. I wish I could tell you that all my mistakes stopped here but they did not.

I moved with some unfinished business, I was still married to Robert. I moved with the understanding that Marcus and I were only friends and that we would maintain that relationship only. You know that did not last long. It was difficult trying to remain friends when we were operating like a family. We did live in different apartments, but we began to develop deeper feelings which led to other things. After God had shown himself to me and helped me so much, I began committing adultery. Some might say it was okay since I was no longer with Robert but I knew that it wasn't.

One night I decided to allow Marcus to sleep over, knowing that I was sinning. Well, that was the longest night of my life. I woke up in the middle of the night feeling like the bed was literally on fire. When I got up out of bed to go to the restroom, I looked in the mirror and saw this face that looked like a monster laughing at me. I had never been so scared before in my life. The next morning he complained that he did not sleep well, so we decided not to stay together any more. We maintained this agreement for awhile. Marcus began having some financial problems and wanted to give up his apartment to move in together. I said no because I knew the curse it would bring. However, over time I gave in.

As soon as we moved in together, things changed. I saw the biggest impact on my finances; I was no longer able to make ends meet even with two incomes in the house. It was like the money was disappearing. I was not ignorant, I knew what was happening; I was living outside of God's will. The worst part is that I knew better. Going to church every Sunday as if we were a family, was a lie. I was still married. I knew what I needed to do; I had to get a divorce immediately. I could not continue to live this way.

While this was happening, I found out that I was pregnant, I was married to one man and pregnant by another. What a mess! I remembered the Sunday we went to church, and the minister preached about living in adultery and shacking. I could not move; I knew that was for us. Now at this point I needed to evaluate this relationship. Where was it going? We talked and Jamal told me that he was ready for marriage. But guess what, I was not. I had just gotten out of a mess. I prayed and asked God. (Why do we ask God for things we really do not want the answer to and then we still do what we want?) God said plainly, "Wait." I questioned wait. I said, "Lord, we have been living together now for a year and I cannot tell him to wait. The children will wonder what is going on."

We got married after the divorce was final. I'm sure you are wondering if we are still married and the answer is, "Yes." So why did God say wait? Because he knew where I was spiritually and emotionally and where Jamal was; we were not equally yoked. I had a lot of extra baggage from the past that I needed to drop. I was not fully healed. It was like reopening a newly healed wound. We were in separate places. Marriage was the last thing I needed.

Trying to recover from all the other bad relationships and operate in a new one was a challenge. I was still trying to find myself spiritually. It was a struggle the first two years. The condemnation I was experiencing for not heeding the word of God was torture. We have made it through, but I see why God said, "Wait." The lesson here: "Please be obedient to God at all cost; he knows so much more than we will ever know." Over time we have learned to pray and study together as a family. The tug of war in the process was not easy. It was not easy for either of us. And even now we have struggles.

I have shared my life with you. This was very difficult to put on paper. I do not want anyone to make the same mistakes I did but if you have, that is okay. Just know that you do not have to stay in the mess that you are in. I have made many mistakes over my lifetime, and several of them I have made repeatedly because of disobedience. At times I blamed my mom for some of my issues. But honestly, she had nothing to do with the choices I made. I knew right from wrong. I have accepted full responsibility for the decisions that I have made on my own. The abuse from my childhood I could not stop, but I cannot allow it to rule over my life.

I want to discourage you from blaming your problems on others. If you are a teen or adult, you have to take responsibility for your part. I do not expect you to take responsibility for another person's action, which is something we have to work through. Focus on what you can change within yourself.

There is so much more of my childhood and life. I was touched inappropriately more often than mentioned in this book. I want you to see where God brought me from and through. If God did it for me, then he can and will do it for you.

Those who know me at work or church would not have guessed my past. I am a living and breathing testimony that God can take your past and transform you into so much more. I would not trade my relationship with God for anything in this world. There is no greater love than the love of Jesus Christ. I have not done anything to deserve his greatness or love. I have given you what God wants you to receive. The number one thing I suggest to whoever is reading this: if you have not accepted Jesus Christ into your life please, do so.

11
I Think I Married The Wrong Man

"The Pharisees also came unto him, tempting him (Jesus), and saying unto him, is it lawful for a man to put away his wife for every cause? And he answered and said unto them, Have ye not read, that he which made them at the beginning made them male and female, And said, For this cause shall a man leave father and mother, and shall cleave to his wife: and they twain shall be one flesh? Wherefore they are no more twain, but one flesh. What therefore God hath joined together, let not man put asunder. They say unto him, why did Moses then command to give a writing of divorcement, and to put her away? He saith unto them, Moses, because of the hardness of your hearts suffered you to put away your wives: but from the beginning it was not so. And I say unto you, whosoever shall put away his wife, except it be for fornication, and shall marry another, committeth adultery: and whoso marrieth her which is put away doth commit adultery." Matthew 19: 3-9

These are Jesus' words, not mine. Before jumping into any marriage or even any relationship, consult your heavenly father and heed to his answer. I asked God for signs prior to my first marriage, and that very next day he gave me three distinct signs. I call the signs "stop signs." The problem was I did not stop. I yielded and proceeded on my own at which time I stepped completely out of God's will. Even after God gave every reason why I should not marry this guy, I decided to ask for advice from a co-worker who encouraged me to do otherwise. The outcome was disaster.

The marriage lasted one year, but we lived together for one month after getting married. There was infidelity on both ends. He started it and I finished it. All I can say is learn from my mistake and take a look at others' mistakes. Since I did not get divorced immediately, I placed others soul in jeopardy by involving them in my sins, having other relationships while married. God intended for marriages to last for eternity, not just years.

I have remarried now and let me tell you it is no picnic. We entered the marriage with the intentions that it would last forever. We were accepting of each other's faults. The number one challenge has been agreeing financially. It is so important to have the Holy Spirit in your marriage. Otherwise, I think I would have left this one. Don't get me wrong, I love my husband but in the past my way of dealing with relationship problems was my way or no way at all. I would just leave. The Holy Spirit will not allow me to do that now. I am very argumentative so I had to learn to be quiet and pray. I seek God in all things now; I mean everything. Being in love is just for the moment, you have to make a righteous decision to love someone if you plan to marry them. I married my current husband knowing that we were unequally yoked, and it has been a challenge. God reminds me that if I am faithful, then my husband will follow. I have to lead by example. I have to live righteous because I have people watching me. If you think you are in a bad marriage, consult Jesus for guidance, not man; this is between you and God.

Why Am I Attracting The Wrong Relationships?

I have asked myself this question over and over again. I have learned that we attract who and what we are. I know it sounds harsh, but that was a realization that I came to see. If you are unstable, then you will attract someone that is unstable. "Why?" you ask. Because when we are in unstable situations such as having an unstable mindset and unstable emotions, we do not think clearly. We follow our hearts, which is very misleading. The Bible says, *"The heart is deceitful above all things, and desperately wicked: who can know it?" Jeremiah 17:9*

When your heart has been broken over and over again, it becomes unhealthy and just as a physically unhealthy heart can kill you, so can an emotionally unhealthy heart. That is why I think that when you have just had a bad break-up or even a divorce, you should wait at least a year before going into another relationship. It gives you time to heal. My recommendation is to give your whole heart to God and he will in exchange give you a new heart. *"A new heart also will I give you, and a new spirit will I put within you: and I will take away the stony heart out of your flesh, and I will give you and heart of flesh." Ezekiel 36:26*

The Effects of Sexual Abuse On My Life

The aftermath of sexual abuse left an enormous toxic residue that led to promiscuity, teenage pregnancy, dropping out of high school, toxic relationships from impaired decision making, a failed marriage, and cycles of physical, emotional, and mental abuse. I contribute my survival to my foundation in church. Although my relationship with God was not as strong as others, I had enough to keep me from drowning in the mess I was in. Do not be fooled, Jesus prays for us daily and that is why we are here. If I had not known God at all, I do not know where I would be today. There were so many times I felt hopeless, worthless, and helpless. I considered taking my life a number of times, but God did not let it happen. Don't ever think that you are in such a mess that God cannot redeem you because he can and he will.

I encountered a number of repercussions after being abused sexually as a child. I had feelings of fear, low self-esteem, inferiority to others, promiscuity, and teen pregnancy. I would never say no when I wanted and needed to. I exposed myself to unhealthy relationships that were oftentimes abusive. I mistook sex for love and intimacy. I had to find out who I was and what my purpose was in life. Something I would like for you to know is that you are precious and great in God's eyes and you are just as important as the next person.

Do not confuse sex with true love and intimacy. You must know that intimacy refers to the feelings of being in a close personal association and belonging together. It is a familiar and very close affective connection with another as a result of entering deeply or closely into relationship through knowledge and experience of the other. Genuine intimacy requires dialogue (talking/conversation/listening), transparency (being completely honest and open), vulnerability (knocking down all walls), and reciprocity (both persons must feel and do the same). If these things do not exist, there is no intimacy and basically no relationship. If you have ever been abused or rejected, you do not have to be a victim of your past. You can overcome. Know and remember who Gods says you are.

Will I Ever Forget and Heal?

You must purpose to put your past to work for you and others. You will not forget your past, so just put it to work. Your past has the power to heal you and others. My past has allowed me to understand the mind of an abuser and the victim; it has allowed me to be able to encourage others and myself. The healing process will not take place overnight. First, you have to make up your mind that you want to make a change. As you can see, I tried to make all sorts of changes that failed. The only sure way to change your situation is to follow after God and accept Jesus Christ into your life. I am not just being religious. It is the truth.

There are things that will and can impede your healing. I was so used to being hurt, I would just wait for it. I became comfortable with pain and rejection. At times it seemed like an addiction. Stop trying to get different results from the same process. Try not to repeat whatever it was that yielded bad results before. Your life just may be a testimony for someone else. And if you are wondering…Why did all this stuff happen to me? Why could my life not be normal like other children/teens my age? God did not predestine your life to be full of mistakes. Unfortunately, the sins of our ancestors and sometimes parents place you in harm's way. The devil tries to destroy our purpose and destiny that is his job, which is why he brings up the past.

"For if you forgive men their trespasses, your heavenly Father will also forgive you. But it you do not forgive men their trespasses, neither will your Father forgive your trespasses." Matthew 6:14-15

Forgiveness is a must, so you ask: How do I forgive a parent who abused me or allowed me to suffer abuse? First and foremost it is a prerequisite in order for Christ to forgive you. I did not say it was easy. It is a process. God loves us all but hates the sin within us. I know the person who abused me. I do not have any contact with him, but he is still around. As a child I can say I was more afraid of him than angry. Fear is the one thing that has ruled me. As for my mother, I disliked the things she did but I always loved her. I was afraid of her, too. I yearned for that mother daughter relationship we never had. I just could not imagine hating my mother. It just did not seem right to me. I took it all to God and left it there. The one thing I can truly say that has still remained is the fear. I discovered that at the time of writing this book.

When I would pray, I felt that there was always something in my heart keeping me from being completely submitted to God. I prayed often to God about the fear in my heart. I prayed and fasted several times but it would still remain. I told God how tired I was of being afraid. In meditating one night, I asked, "Where did this fear come from?" He replied, "From your youth."

One of my fears just happens to be writing all this. What will people think? Will church people condemn me? Will someone have a problem with my views? Well, if you are reading this I have overcome. If you do not deal with and conquer your past, it will continue to rule over you. It is not worth it. Forgive whoever hurt you.

Now you have to take your life out of your hand. What do I mean? If you have not already accepted Jesus Christ into your life, now is the time. Begin the healing process. After that make a practice/habit of reading God's word every day. In his Word he will begin to reveal to you, who you are in him. Counseling without Jesus Christ is useless.

"Father, I know that I have broken your laws and my sins have separated me from you. I am truly sorry, and now I want to turn away from my past sinful life toward you. Please forgive me, and help me avoid sinning again. I believe that your son, Jesus Christ, died for my sins, was resurrected from the dead, is alive, and hears my prayer. I invite Jesus to become the Lord of my life, to rule and reign in my heart from this day forward. Please send your Holy Spirit to help me obey you, and to do your will for the rest of my life. In Jesus name I pray, Amen."

12
No More Tears

I allowed the devil to remind me of my past and bring it forward. I started bringing my yesterday into my today. I have to remember that yesterday is where and who I was and today is who and where I am. Tomorrow is where I am going. I am birthing my purpose. When we hold on to past failures, this leads to anger, hate, bitterness, and rejection, which lays a foundation and continues to remind us of why we are hurt and angry. If you are like me, you may need a step-by-step process. These are the steps God has given me:

- If you have not accepted Jesus Christ as Lord and Savior into your life, then you must. I will not allow anyone to think that we can do anything without God; it's not possible. God made you, and he knows your purpose better than you.
- Forgive yourself and everyone who has hurt you. One of the most fulfilling things for me has been learning to love my enemies and those that hurt me. It feels great once you know who you are in God. For all your mistakes, this is a must. If God can forgive you, then who are you to hold on to it?
- Be thankful. Lord, I thank you for making me who I am. I know God did not make a mistake in making and shaping me.
- Read God's Word and pray daily
- Ask God to show you your purpose and walk in it.
- Find a church home.

I could have allowed all the hurt I saw my mother experience in church hinder me, but something in me would not allow that. The purpose of fellowship is to refuel you and when you are refueled, you have an obligation to take it to someone outside the church. I have made a righteous decision to serve God. I would not trade it for anything in this world. If you do not take anything else from this book, please take Jesus; that's the best I have to offer! He is great! I know because I tried him. May God bless you!

www.ingramcontent.com/pod-product-compliance
Lightning Source LLC
Chambersburg PA
CBHW071012120726
47910CB00004B/1484